"十三五"国家重点出版规划项目

李白诗歌全集英译

A Complete Edition of Pai Li's Poems in Chinese and English
With Annotations

赵彦春 译·注

Translated and Annotated by Yanchun Chao

第八卷

Volume VIII

上海大学出版社
·上海·

卷 八

目 录
Contents

1719 **古近体诗六十五首**
Old-new Rhythmic Poetry, 65 Poems

1721 越中秋怀
An Impromptu of Autumn in Mid-Yüeh

1723 效古二首
Learning from the Past, Two Poems

1728 拟古十二首
Imitation of Ancients, Twelve Poems

1749 感兴八首
Observations, Eight Poems

1764 寓言三首
Three Fables

1769 秋夕旅怀
Touched While Travelling at Dusk in Autumn

1771 感遇四首
Touched, Four Poems

1776 翰林读书言怀呈集贤诸学士
Expressing My Will to the Scholars When Reading in Brushwood

1778 寻阳紫极宫感秋作
Touched at the Autumn View at Purple Palace in Bankshine

1780 江上秋怀
An Impromptu of Autumn on the River

1782 秋夕书怀
Expressing Myself at Dusk in Autumn

1784	避地司空原言怀	
	Retiring to Mt. Ssukung	
1787	上崔相百忧章（时在浔阳狱）	
	Writing to Premier Ts'ui to Vent My Rues (Jailed in Bankshine)	
1791	万愤词投魏郎中	
	To Way, the Royal Guard, to Vent My Anger	
1795	荆州贼平临洞庭言怀作	
	Expressing My Anger at Cavehall When Rebels Are Wiped Out in Chaste	
1798	览镜书怀	
	An Impromptu When Looking into a Mirror	
1799	田园言怀	
	On a Farmland	
1800	江南春怀	
	A Spring Impromptu in the South	
1801	听蜀僧濬弹琴	
	Listening to a Monk from Shu Play the Lute	
1802	鲁东门观刈蒲	
	Watching Reaping of Cattail to the East of Gate of Lu	
1804	咏邻女东窗海石榴	
	Ode to the Girl Neighbor by the Sea Pomegranate at Her East Window	
1806	南轩松	
	A Pine by South Window	
1807	咏山樽二首	
	Ode to the Wooden Cup, Two Poems	
1809	初出金门寻王侍御不遇，咏壁上鹦鹉	
	Ode to the Parrot on the Wall When I Fail to See Wang, the Royal Servant, Soon After My Being Exiled	
1810	紫藤树	
	Wistaria	
1811	观放白鹰二首	
	Watching the White Hawk, Two Poems	

1813	观博平王志安少府山水粉图
	Appreciating the Mountain-River Water Color Painting of Chih-an Wang, Magistrate of Broadpeace
1814	题雍丘崔明府丹灶
	An Inscription for Red Forge of Ts'ui, Magistrate of Pondknoll
1816	观元丹丘坐巫山屏风
	Watching Redknoll Yüan Sitting Before a Screen of Mt. Witch
1818	求崔山人百丈崖瀑布图
	Asking for a Highcliff-Waterfall Painting from Ts'ui, the Hermit
1820	见野草中有白头翁者
	Windflowers Appear in the Grass
1821	流夜郎题葵叶
	Inscription for a Mallow Leaf in Nightboy
1822	莹禅师房观山海图
	Viewing the Painting of Mountains and Seas in Ying's Zen Room
1824	白鹭鸶
	The White Egret
1825	咏槿
	Ode to the Hibiscus
1826	咏桂
	Ode to the Laurel
1828	白胡桃
	A White Chestnut
1829	巫山枕障
	Mt. Witch Painted on the Screen
1830	南奔书怀
	An Impromptu While I Flee Down South

1835 **古近体诗八十八首**
Old-new Rhythmic Poetry, 88 Poems

1837 题随州紫阳先生壁
Inscription for the Wall of Purple Sun from Suichow

1839	题元丹丘山居
	Inscription for Redknoll Yüan's Abode in the Mountains

1841	题元丹丘颖阳山居
	Inscription for Redknoll Yüan's Abode in the Mountains in Yingshine

1843	题瓜洲新河饯族叔舍人贲
	Inscription for the New Canal in Melon Shoal While Feasting Fen, My Uncle, the Royal Servant

1845	洗脚亭
	Washing Feet by the Pavilion

1847	劳劳亭
	The Farewell Pavilion

1848	题金陵王处士水亭
	Inscription for the Water Pavilion of Wang, a Hermit, in Gold Hill

1850	题嵩山逸人元丹丘山居
	Inscription for the Mountain Abode of Redknoll Yüan, a Hermit on Mt. Tower

1854	题江夏修静寺
	Inscription for Quietude Fane in Riversummer

1856	改九子山为九华山联句
	A Cooperation on a Verse for Mt. Nine Sons Changed Into Mt. Nine Flowers

1858	题宛溪馆
	Inscription for Wan Stream Mansion

1860	题东溪公幽居
	Inscription for Lord East Stream's Villa

1861	嘲鲁儒
	Sneering at a Lu Confucian

1863	惧谗
	Fear for Slander

1865	观猎
	Watching Hunting

1867	观胡人吹笛
	Watching the Hun Man Playing the Pipe

1869	军行	
	The General	
1870	从军行	
	A War Poem	
1871	平虏将军妻	
	Beat Foe General's Wife	
1872	春夜洛城闻笛	
	Listening to the Flute in Loshine on a Spring Night	
1873	嵩山采菖蒲者	
	A Bulrush Gatherer on Mt. Tower	
1875	金陵听韩侍御吹笛	
	Listening to Han, the Royal Servant, Who Plays the Pipe in Gold Hill	
1877	流夜郎闻酺不预	
	Exiled in Nightboy and Unable to Attend a Symposium	
1878	放后遇恩不沾	
	Exiled and Not Pardoned	
1879	宣城见杜鹃花	
	Seeing Azaleas in Hsuan	
1880	白田马上闻莺	
	Hearing Orioles Chirp on My Horse at White Field	
1882	三五七言	
	Three, Five and Seven Words	
1883	杂诗	
	Miscellany	
1885	寄远	
	Missing Her Afar	
1903	长信宫	
	Long Faith Palace	
1905	长门怨二首	
	Plaint in Long Gate Hall, Two Poems	
1907	春怨	
	Plaint in Spring	

1908	代赠远	
	To Whom Afar in My Wife's Voice	
1910	陌上赠美人	
	To the Beauty on the Lane	
1911	闺情	
	A Lady's Rue	
1913	代别情人	
	Seeing Off Husband in My Wife's Voice	
1915	代秋情	
	Autumn Rue in My Wife's Voice	
1917	对酒	
	Drinking Wine	
1918	怨情	
	The Plaint	
1920	湖边采莲妇	
	A Woman Gathering Lotus Pods on the Lake	
1921	怨情	
	The Plaint	
1922	代寄情楚词体	
	A Plaint in My Wife's Voice, in the Style of Ch'u Lyrics	
1924	学古思边	
	Thinking of the Border like Ancients	
1926	思边	
	Thinking of the Border	
1927	口号吴王美人半醉	
	Making Fun of King of Wu's Beauty, Who Is Half Drunk, an Oral Impromptu	
1928	代美人愁镜	
	Her Sadness in the Mirror	
1932	赠段七娘	
	To Tuan, Sis Seven	
1933	别内赴征三首	
	Farewell to My Wife to Join the Army, Three Poems	

1936	秋浦寄内
	To My Wife in Autumn Shoal
1938	自代内赠
	A Gift in My Wife's Voice
1941	秋浦感主人归燕寄内
	Sending My Wife a Letter When Moved by the Leaving Swallow from My Host's House in Autumn Shore
1943	送内寻庐山女道士李腾空二首
	Sending My Wife to Look for Miss Leap-to-Soar, a Woman Hermit in Mt. Lodge, Two Poems
1945	赠内
	To My Wife
1946	在浔阳非所寄内
	A Letter to My Wife When I'm Jailed in Bankshine
1948	南流夜郎寄内
	A Letter to My Wife While I'm Exiled South in Nightboy
1949	越女词五首
	Five Lyrics on the Yüeh Girl
1954	浣纱石上女
	The Lass on the Yarn Washing Stone
1955	示金陵子
	To the Courtesan in Gold Hill
1957	出妓金陵子呈卢六四首
	A Singing Girl in Gold Hill, to Lu Six, Four Poems
1961	巴女词
	Words of a Wife from Pa
1962	哭晁卿衡
	Mourning Heng Ch'ao, a Japanese Friend
1963	自溧水道哭王炎
	Mourning Yan Wang in the Town of Li River
1967	哭宣城善酿纪叟
	Mourning Old Chi, a Good Brewer in Hsuan

1968 宣城哭蒋徵君华
Wailing Hua Chiang the Recruit in Hsuan

1971 **拾遗六十四首**
Gleanings, 64 Poems

1973 杂言用投丹阳知己兼奉宣慰判官
A Few Words to My Friend in Redshine, an Assistant Official for Publicity

1975 南陵五松山别荀七
Farewell to Hsun Seven at Mt. Five Pines in Southridge

1977 观鱼潭
Watching Fish in a Pondlet

1978 自广平乘醉走马六十里至邯郸登城楼览古书怀
An Impromptu on the Wall Tower of Hantan After Travelling Twenty Miles from Broadpeace While Drunk Astride My Horse

1983 月夜金陵怀古
My Moonlit Recall of the Past in Gold Hill

1985 金陵新亭
Kiosk New in Gold Hill

1986 庭前晚开花
It Blooms Late in My Yard

1987 宣州长史弟昭赠余琴谿中双舞鹤诗以见志
Secretary of Hsuan's Brother Gives Me a Pair of Cranes Called Lute Stream, So I Compose This Poem to Express My Gratitude

1989 暖酒
Warming Wine

1990 戏赠杜甫
A Poem to Fu Tu for Fun

1991 寒女吟
A Sad Wife's Croon

1993 会别离
Hope for a Reunion

1995	初月	
	The Crescent	
1996	雨后望月	
	Looking at the Moon After a Rain	
1997	对雨	
	Facing the Rain	
1998	晓晴	
	Clearing Up at Dawn	
1999	望夫石	
	The O-Come-Hubby Stone	
2001	冬日归旧山	
	Returning to the Old Hills on a Winter Day	
2004	邹衍谷	
	Yan Tsou's Dale	
2005	入清溪行山中	
	Boating on a Brook in the Mountains	
2006	日出东南隅行	
	The Sun Rises in the Southeast	
2007	代佳人寄翁参枢先辈	
	To Respected Ts'anshu Weng in My Wife's Words	
2008	送客归吴	
	Seeing Off My Guest to Wu	
2009	送友生游峡中	
	Seeing Off My Friend to Tour the Gorge	
2011	送袁明府任长沙	
	Seeing Off Magistrate Yüan to Govern Long Sand	
2013	送史司马赴崔相公幕	
	Seeing Off Commander Shih to Serve Under Premier Ts'ui	
2015	战城南	
	Fighting South of the Town	
2017	胡无人行	
	Hun，There Will Be None	

2018	鞠歌行	
	A Football Song	
2020	题许宣平庵壁	
	An Inscription for the Wall of Hsu's Temple	
2021	题峰顶寺	
	An Inscription for Temple on the Peak	
2022	题舒州司空山瀑布	
	An Inscription for Mt. Ssukung Waterfalls in Shuchow	
2023	断句	
	Fragments	
2025	阳春曲	
	A Tune of Sunny Spring	
2026	舍利佛	
	Sariputra	
2027	摩多楼子	
	Mordor Tower	
2028	春感	
	Feeling the Spring	
2030	殷十一赠栗冈砚	
	Yin Eleven Gives Me a Chestnut Mound Slab	
2032	普照寺	
	All Glare Temple	
2033	钓台	
	Fishing Platform	
2034	小桃源	
	A Small Fairyland	
2035	题窦圌山	
	An Inscription for Mt. T'uan Tou	
2036	赠江油尉	
	To the Sheriff of Riveroil	
2038	清平乐	
	Pure Peace Tune	

2042	清平乐令	
	Pure Peace Tune	
2045	桂殿秋	
	Autumn in Laurel Hall	
2047	连理枝	
	Twigs Entwined	
2050	杂题	
	Miscellanies	
2054	立冬	
	Beginning of Winter	
2055	上清宝鼎诗二首	
	Celestial Tripod, Two Poems	
2060	白微时	
	When I Was Low	
2061	夜宿山寺	
	Putting Up for the Night in a Mountain Temple	
2062	题戴老酒店	
	An Inscription for Mr. Tai's Wineshop	
2063	折荷有赠	
	Plucking a Lotus Bloom as a Gift	
2064	别匡山	
	Good-bye to Mt. Square	
2065	**译者简介**	
	About the Translator	

古近体诗六十五首
Old-new Rhythmic Poetry, 65 Poems

越 中 秋 怀

越水绕碧山,
周回数千里。
乃是天镜中,
分明画相似。
爱此从冥搜,
永怀临湍游。
一为沧波客,
十见红蕖秋。
观涛壮天险,
望海令人愁。
路遐迫西照,
岁晚悲东流。
何必探禹穴,
逝将归蓬丘。
不然五湖上,
亦可乘扁舟。

An Impromptu of Autumn in Mid-Yüeh

The Yüeh does the hills there surround,
And zigzags a thousand miles round.
Behold, Heaven's Mirror it is!
And a painting is just like this.
The secrecy I would explore,
And tour while the river does pour.
A hermit, here and there I go,

Ten times I've seen lotuses blow.
I see the tide surge to the sky,
And gazing at the sea I sigh.
It's a long way! The late sun glows.
Late in the year, the stream east flows!
Worm's Cave, why should I look inside?
On the Thistle Knoll I'd abide,
Or in the Five Lakes I may row,
Chasing the waves with my canoe.

* Mid-Yüeh: today's Shaohsing, Chechiang Province.
* the Yüeh: the Yüeh River, probably referring to the O Ts'ao River, a branch of the Ch'ient'ang River.
* Worm's Cave: a cave in Mt. Summit, where Worm was buried.
* the Thistle Knoll: unidentified, probably a metaphor in this poem because the Thistle Knoll is the name of a fairy mountain.
* the Five Lakes: referring to Grand Lake (Lake T'ai) and the other four smaller lakes around. As legend goes, Li Fan (536 B.C.- 448 B.C.), a renowned statesman, strategist, economist and Wordist in the Spring and Autumn period, changed his name to live in seclusion among the five lakes after he helped the State of Yüeh wipe out Wu.

效 古 二 首

Learning from the Past, Two Poems

其 一

朝入天苑中,
谒帝蓬莱宫。
青山映辇道,
碧树摇烟空。
谬题金闺籍,
得与银台通。
待诏奉明主,
抽毫颂清风。
归时落日晚,
踯躅浮云骢。
人马本无意,
飞驰自豪雄。
入门紫鸳鸯,
金井双梧桐。
清歌弦古曲,
美酒沽新丰。
快意且为乐,
列筵坐群公。
光景不可留,
生世如转蓬。
早达胜晚遇,
羞比垂钓翁。

No. 1

I come to Heaven's Park at dawn,
And Fairyland Hall I'll call on.
The blue hills shade the Sedan Way;
The luxuriant trees in mist sway.
Gold Book Hall may admit a scum,
So to Silver Gate I oft come.
I'll serve His Majesty divine
And write to praise government fine.
My return sees the setting sun,
And my piebald trots up to run.
People or steeds don't want to vie;
They may run fast as if to fly.
Into the gate mandarin ducks go;
By Gold Well two phoenix trees grow.
The old tune goes with the strings fine;
Newrich does offer the best wine.
In life, go merry while we may;
At feast with grandees we should play.
Time we can't keep howe'er we try;
Life's short as thistledown does fly.
We'd gain as early as we can,
Unlike Chiang, the old fishing man.

* Heaven's Park: the royal Forbidden Park.
* Fairyland Hall: what was later called Great Bright Palace.
* Gold Book Hall: a royal hall in which hung were books of names that could enter the palace.
* Silver Gate: a palace gate close to Brushwood Academy.
* Newrich: a county, known for wine brewed there. The county was built by Pang Liu in

imitation of his hometown Rich County. Newrich is in today's Lintung County, near Hsi-an, Sha'anhsi Province. Pang Liu, Emperor Highsire, born in Rich, rose from grassroots, wiped out Hsiang's army and established Han, with Long Peace as its capital. As his father missed the beauty and wine of his hometown, Pang Liu made a copy of his hometown and moved the best brewers here, and ever since then Newrich wine has been well-known, attracting generations of litterateurs to sing praise of it.

* thistledown: the pappus of a thistle; the ripe silky fibers from the dry flower of a thistle, a metaphor for aimless drifting or wandering of a vagrant.
* Chiang: referring to Tseya Chiang, also known as Great Grand, an influential strategist and statesman. Though he was a butcher at his young age, Great Grand remained diligent in hardship, expecting to display his ability for the country one day, but he did not make any achievement before he was 70 years old. He went west at the age of 72, fishing as he waited for King Civil, and finally won his appreciation.

其 二

自古有秀色,
西施与东邻。
蛾眉不可妒,
况乃效其颦。
所以尹婕妤,
羞见邢夫人。
低头不出气,
塞默少精神。
寄语无盐子,
如君何足珍。

No. 2

There're shining beauties as of yore;
Miss West and Miss East were next door.
Towering brows cannot be pulled down;
Can East mimic West with her frown?
So Yin, Court Concubine so fair,
Could not with Lady Hsing compare.
She held her breath and bent her head;
Low and listless, nothing she said.
To No Salt I give my advice:
What is your worth? What is your price?

* Miss West: West Maid, one of the most beautiful women in Chinese history.
* Miss East: East Maid, Miss West's ugly neighbor, who was sneered at for having mimicked West Maid's frowning because she looked even uglier when frowning.
* Yin: Emperor Martial's imperial concubine.

* No Salt: name of a virtuous but ugly woman from a fief called No Salt, or referring to any ugly woman.
* Lady Hsing: Emperor Martial's lady, whose status was higher than imperial concubines. Lady Hsing was higher in status and more beautiful than Yin, the imperial concubine.

拟 古 十 二 首
Imitation of Ancients, Twelve Poems

其 一

青天何历历，
明星如白石。
黄姑与织女，
相去不盈尺。
银河无鹊桥，
非时将安适。
闺人理纨素，
游子悲行役。
瓶冰知冬寒，
霜露欺远客。
客似秋叶飞，
飘摇不言归。
别后罗带长，
愁宽去时衣。
乘月托宵梦，
因之寄金徽。

No. 1

In the blue sky, all stars shine bright,
The brightest one like a stone white.
Lo, Weaver Maid and Yellow May
Are close friends, a few feet away.
There is no Magpie Bridge there now;

How to cross the Milky Way, how?
The wife is busy on the loom;
The vagrant drifts along in gloom.
The ice in the vase coldness knows;
The frost with the dew bullies toes.
A vagrant is a leaf that flies,
No home to go beneath the skies.
I have grown thin since our good bye;
My gown becomes loose by and by.
The moon hastens my dream, alas,
To the border and to the pass.

* Weaver Maid: Vega, a fairy who loved Cowherd and was married to him in Chinese mythology. Weaver Maid was taken away and kept away from Cowherd by Queen Mother, and she stayed on the other side of the Silver River (the Milky Way) Queen Mother made with her hair pin.
* Yellow May: Altair, mentioned in some literature but not specific, probably Cowherd's real name.
* Magpie Bridge: the bridge where Weaver Maid and Cowherd meet once a year on the seventh day of the seventh moon. The bridge was built with twigs by magpies that sympathized with Weaver Maid and Cowherd so that they could meet once a year.
* the Milky Way: the Silver River that Queen Mother made with her hair pin in Chinese mythology; a luminous band circling the heavens composed of stars and nebulae; the Galaxy.

其 二

高楼入青天，
下有白玉堂。
明月看欲堕，
当窗悬清光。
遥夜一美人，
罗衣沾秋霜。
含情弄柔瑟，
弹作陌上桑。
弦声何激烈，
风卷绕飞梁。
行人皆踯躅，
栖鸟起回翔。
但写妾意苦，
莫辞此曲伤。
愿逢同心者，
飞作紫鸳鸯。

No. 2

The tower scrapes the blue sky, so tall;
There stands below a White Jade Hall.
Will it fall down, the moon so bright?
It floods the window with pure light.
A belle, in her sleepless night lost,
Feels cold, her clothes frozen with frost.
Amorous, the lute she does play,
And sings the *Lane Mulberry* lay.
How plaintive, how sad are the strings!

Around the beams her sadness rings.
A passer-by hangs on, alack;
The birds perching fly and turn back.
It's me that suffers bitter pain,
So that there rings a painful strain.
How I wish a true friend came by
So, like mandarin ducks, we could fly!

* White Jade Hall: an allusion to two lines of an old poem—Bright gold is your gate; white jade is your hall.
* *Lane Mulberry*: an ancient poem that has been popular since the Han dynasty.
* mandarin ducks: web-footed, short-legged, broad-billed water birds that always appear in loving pairs, a metaphor for couples in Chinese culture.

其 三

长绳难系日，
自古共悲辛。
黄金高北斗，
不惜买阳春。
石火无留光，
还如世中人。
即事已如梦，
后来我谁身。
提壶莫辞贫，
取酒会四邻。
仙人殊恍惚，
未若醉中真。

No. 3

A rope, tho long, can't the sun tie;
As e'er, at this people can but sigh.
With gold piled like the Dipper high,
An inch of spring one could not buy.
The stone fire will soon disappear,
Like people in the dust world here.
Life is like a dream, a dream be!
What will happen then after me?
Take your pot, be free as you dine;
Do invite your neighbors to wine!
Immortals are so vague, like fog;

Do drink and lie drunk, a dead log.

* the Dipper: a constellation composed of seven bright stars, which looks like a spoon in the sky; sometimes used as a metaphor for a guide.

其 四

清都绿玉树，
灼烁瑶台春。
攀花弄秀色，
远赠天仙人。
香风送紫蕊，
直到扶桑津。
取掇世上艳，
所贵心之珍。
相思传一笑，
聊欲示情亲。

No. 4

The clean town, the emerald trees;
The glory of spring Jade Mound sees.
I pluck and wave a blushing spray
For the immortal far away.
The wind sends petals to beguile
Those in the Fairyland and Isle.
In the world pluck the blossoms best
And hold it with love on your chest.
Missing you, I'd send you a smile
So I could be calmed for a while.

* Jade Mound: one of the twelve jade mounds on Mt. Queen, each a thousand feet wide with five colors of jade as their base.
* the Fairyland and Isle: a legendary place on East Sea, where twin mulberry trees can grow as tall as 6,600 meters in height and 6,600 meters in girth, and where the sun rises.

其 五

今日风日好，
明日恐不如。
春风笑于人，
何乃愁自居。
吹箫舞彩凤，
酌醴鲙神鱼。
千金买一醉，
取乐不求余。
达士遗天地，
东门有二疏。
愚夫同瓦石，
有才知卷舒。
无事坐悲苦，
块然涸辙鱼。

No. 5

Today, it is a good nice day;
Will tomorrow come the same way?
The spring wind smiles, as if so glad;
But I live all alone, how sad!
The flute's played for a phoenix swish;
The cup's filled to go with best fish.
To be drunk, I'd spend all my gold;
So happy, what more need I hold?
Real talents tour Heaven and earth;
Two Shus left the court for real worth.
A fool is stiff like bricks and tiles;

>A sage holds all sizes and styles.
>Don't sigh helplessly, therein shut,
>Like the fish so mad in the rut.

* phoenix: a legendary bird of great beauty, unique of its kind, which was supposed to live five or six hundred years before consuming itself by fire, rising again from its ashes to live through another cycle, a symbol of immortality. In Chinese mythology, the phoenix only perches on phoenix trees, i.e. firmiana, only eats firmiana fruit, and only drinks sweet spring water, and this mythic bird appears only in times of peace and sagacious rule.
* Two Shus: two worthy brothers in the Han dynasty and Shu is their family name.

其 六

运速天地闭，
胡风结飞霜。
百草死冬月，
六龙颓西荒。
太白出东方，
彗星扬精光。
鸳鸯非越鸟，
何为眷南翔。
惟昔鹰将犬，
今为侯与王。
得水成蛟龙，
争池夺凤凰。
北斗不酌酒，
南箕空簸扬。

No. 6

Heaven and earth are overcast;
A northern wind whirls frost so fast.
All grasses suffer the cold spell;
Six-Dragons sets beyond the dell.
Venus appears in the east, bright;
A comet shoots forth dazzling light.
From south mandarin ducks are not;
Why do they miss South Land a lot?
Then the dogs and hawks did wild sway;
Now they hold power as lords today.
For water all dragons hard vie;

To gain the most, their best they try.
The Dipper, cup-like, holds no wine;
The Dustpan, called pan, can't incline.

* Six-dragons: alias of the sun.
* Venus: In Chinese astrology, there will be a disaster when Venus shows up across the sky in the daytime.
* South Land: the land south of the Yangtze River generally from Nanking to Shanghai, which is the estuary.
* mandarin ducks: duck-like love birds that appear in pairs, a metaphor for couples in Chinese culture.
* the Dipper: a constellation composed of seven bright stars, which looks like a spoon in the sky.
* the Dustpan: referring to Cepheus, a northern constellation near Draco and Cassiopeia.

其 七

世路今太行，
回车竟何托。
万族皆凋枯，
遂无少可乐。
旷野多白骨，
幽魂共销铄。
荣贵当及时，
春华宜照灼。
人非昆山玉，
安得长璀错？
身没期不朽，
荣名在麟阁。

No. 7

The roads are hard, so hard they are!
How can I on them drive my car?
All races age and cease to be;
As e'er, nobody has much glee.
Many white bones in the field lie;
Even ghosts and souls will all die.
We'd be rich and merry in time,
Like the spring blossoms in their prime.
Humans are Mt. Queen jade there;
How can they gleam for long, for e'er.
Tho dead, they may pass on their fame;
As with pride they have carved their name.

* Mt. Queen jade: jade from Mt. Queen, the best jade and most beautiful of all kinds of jade, a metaphor for a brilliant talent.
* with pride they have carved their name: referring to generals who have sacrificed their lives for the country. Emperor Hsuan of Han had martyrs painted and hung in Unicorn Hall in memory of their merits.

其 八

月色不可扫，
客愁不可道。
玉露生秋衣，
流萤飞百草。
日月终销毁，
天地同枯槁。
蟪蛄啼青松，
安见此树老。
金丹宁误俗，
昧者难精讨。
尔非千岁翁，
多恨去世早。
饮酒入玉壶，
藏身以为宝。

No. 8

The moonshine one cannot sweep off;
My worries I can hardly doff.
The dewdrops do my clothes harass;
The fire worms fly over the grass.
No sun or moon can for e'er stay;
Heaven and earth will both decay.
Cicadas in the pine trees shrill;
So sad, the trees age, and they will.
E'en if elixir ne'er e'er kills,
One can't cure folly with such pills.
Since an immortal you are not,

Your death you'd not grudge a lot.
Your wine kettle you should cherish;
And stay in it ere you perish.

* fire worm: also called firefly, any of a family (Lampyridae) of winged beetles, active at night, whose abdomens usually glow with a luminescent light.
* cicada: a homopterous insect that sings its song of summer and shrills in autumn, a symbol of death and resurrection in Chinese culture because of its metamorphosis and recycle. Therefore, in ancient China, a jade cicada figure was put in the mouth of a dead body with such an intention of eternal life.
* stay in it ere you perish: The poet alluded to a story, which is like this: Ch'angfang Fei, a market monitor, once saw an old man selling medicine, his kettle hung at the entrance of the market. When business was over, the old man jumped into his kettle.

其 九

生者为过客，
死者为归人。
天地一逆旅，
同悲万古尘。
月兔空捣药，
扶桑已成薪。
白骨寂无言，
青松岂知春。
前后更叹息，
浮荣何足珍？

No. 9

The living are but passers-by;
The dead are those who passed away.
The world's an inn twixt earth and sky;
Sadly, all people will turn clay.
Moon Hare makes elixir in vain;
The fairy trees turn into wood.
White bones have nothing to complain;
Green pines know not spring warmly good.
The future like the past will perish;
Fame and ranks one should not cherish.

* the fairy trees: referring to twin mulberries on legendary Fairyland or Fairy Isles on East Sea, which grow entwined with each other, as tall as 6,600 meters in height and 6,600 meters in girth.
* Moon Hare: In Chinese myths, there is a hare on the moon ramming elixir. And because of this, the moon is also called Jade Hare in Chinese culture.

其 十

仙人骑彩凤,
昨下阆风岑。
海水三清浅,
桃源一见寻。
遗我绿玉杯,
兼之紫琼琴。
杯以倾美酒,
琴以闲素心。
二物非世有,
何论珠与金。
琴弹松里风,
杯劝天上月。
风月长相知,
世人何倏忽。

No. 10

The saint does a hued phoenix ride,
Having come down Mt. Lang's side.
Thrice you've seen drying of the sea;
Once in Peach Blossoms you've met me.
You gave me a cup of jade made
And a lute that's with jewels inlaid.
The cup full of wine will me please;
The lute well plucked sets me at ease.
These two, not from the world, are rare;
Can pearls or gold with them compare?
While pine trees sough, the lute I play;

With the cup, I greet Luna: pray!
The moon or wind is my best friend;
Life so short, very soon it'll end.

* Mt. Lang: a ridge on Mt. Queen.
* Peach Blossoms: Peach Blossom Source. According to Yüanming Tao's writing, a group of Ch'in people fled to Peach Blossom Source to keep away from the turbulent days, and the people and their offsprings had lived an idyllic and isolated life for 500 years before a fisherman of Chin stumbled into the village.
* pearl: a lustrous, calcareous concretion deposited in layers around a central nucleus in the shells of various mollusks, and largely used as a gem or regarded as a treasure or given as a gift to represent love and friendship.
* Luna: an important image in Chinese literature. A Chinese poet like Pai Li will always invite the moon to have a drink.

其十一

涉江弄秋水，
爱此荷花鲜。
攀荷弄其珠，
荡漾不成圆。
佳人彩云里，
欲赠隔远天。
相思无由见，
怅望凉风前。

No. 11

I wade while with water I play,
And love the lotus blossoms gay.
A leaf pulled, I turn a dew drop;
The ripple's not a circle, slop!
The belle is on the cloud so high;
I can't greet her, barred by the sky.
I miss you: Can I see you, where?
In the cold sough, I blankly stare.

* lotus: one of the various plants of the waterlily family, noted for their large floating leaves and showy flowers, an important image in Chinese culture; in most cases it is associated with Buddhism, for example, Pai Li has various names, one of which is Green Lotus Buddhist.

其十二

去去复去去，
辞君还忆君。
汉水既殊流，
楚山亦此分。
人生难称意，
岂得长为群。
越燕喜海日，
燕鸿思朔云。
别久容华晚，
琅玕不能饭。
日落知天昏，
梦长觉道远。
望夫登高山，
化石竟不返。

No. 12

Go and go, more I go and go;
As I leave you, more I miss you.
The Han divides itself to pour;
Mt. Ch'u has not one peak but more.
In life no one could be best done;
How can we stay for long as one?
Swallows love the sunlit ocean;
Wild geese miss north clouds in motion.
Since parting, we've aged a great deal;
Pearls and jewels can't serve as a meal.
Now it's dark as set has the sun;

Our dream's long, our way a long one.
Husband! Uphill I gaze alone!
You ne'er come back, now a stone.

* the Han: the Han River, the longest tributary of the Long River, which originates in Sha'ahsi and flows southwestward through Hupei, joining the main stream at Hankow, one of the three towns of present-day Wuhan.
* Mt. Ch'u: usually known as Mt. Chaste, on the west bank of the Han River, in the west of today's Hupei Province.
* swallow: a passerine black bird, with short broad, depressed bill, long pointed wings, and forked tail, noted for fleeting flight and migratory habits. In Chinese culture, swallows are welcome to live with a family with their nest on a beam.
* wild goose: an undomesticated goose that is caring and responsible, taken as a symbol of benevolence, righteousness, good manner, wisdom, and faith in Chinese culture.
* pearl: a smooth, lustrous, usually white and bluish-gray, calcareous concretion deposited in layers around a central nucleus in the shells of various mollusks or oysters, and largely used as a gem, medicine or given as a gift, a metaphor for the dearest one, a representation of nobility, purity and dignity in Chinese culture.

感 兴 八 首

Observations, Eight Poems

其 一

瑶姬天帝女，
精彩化朝云。
宛转入宵梦，
无心向楚君。
锦衾抱秋月，
绮席空兰芬。
茫昧竟谁测？
虚传宋玉文。

No. 1

Jade Girl, daughter of God of Sky
Became a hued cloud in the blue.
She into my dream does oft pry,
I will not serve the Lord of Ch'u.
The silk quilt does the moon caress;
The orchid on the mat looks chaste.
Who in the dark there makes a guess?
Jade Sung's poems are over praised.

* Jade Girl: referring to Goddess of Mt. Witch, a beautiful fairy dwelling in Mt. Witch, who shaped herself as clouds at dawn and turned into rain at dusk. In myths, King Huai of Ch'u once met her in his dream, and had an intercourse overnight. The story was recorded by Jade Sung, a student of Yüan Ch'ü's, when he travelled to Cloud Dream Moor with King Hsiang.

* orchid: a terrestrial or epiphytic monocotyledonous plant having thickened bulbous roots and often very showy distinctive flowers, one of the four most important floral images in Chinese literature, which are wintersweet, orchid, bamboo, and chrysanthemum.
* Jade Sung: Jade Sung (cir. 298 B.C.- cir. 222 B.C.), a student of Yüan Ch'ü's, and a verse writer in the Warring States period. He once served as an official for King Hsiang of Ch'u.

其 二

洛浦有宓妃，
飘飖雪争飞。
轻云拂素月，
了可见清辉。
解佩欲西去，
含情讵相违。
香尘动罗袜，
绿水不沾衣。
陈王徒作赋，
神女岂同归？
好色伤大雅，
多为世所讥。

No. 2

Near the Lo lives one called Moon Girl,
Around whom snow flies in a whirl.
She is like fleece and like a beam;
Her skin sheds a translucent gleam.
She doffs her pendant and goes west;
How can I check her with love blessed?
The balmy dust does her socks stir;
The dew wets not the clothes on her.
In vain Chih Ts'ao did verse compose;
How could Goddess look at his prose?
Too much lust destroys taste and grace,
Much laughed at by the human race.

* the Lo: the Lo River, which originates from the south foot of Mt. Flora, flows through the ancient capital Loshine and into the Yellow River. It is one of the progenitors of Chinese civilization.
* Moon Girl: a spirit or Goddess of the Lo River.
* Chih Ts'ao: Chih Ts'ao (A.D. 192 - A.D. 232), Making by courtesy name, Ts'ao Ts'ao's third son, a famous litterateur, a representative of Making Peace Literature. His *Verse to Moon Girl* has been best remembered throughout history.

其 三

裂素持作书,
将寄万里怀。
眷眷待远信,
竟岁无人来。
征鸿务随阳,
又不为我栖。
委之在深箧,
蠹鱼坏其题。
何如投水中,
流落他人开。
不惜他人开,
但恐生是非。

No. 3

On the cloth I write and write on;
I'll send it off to my dear one.
For the messenger long I wait;
None's come till the year's o'er, so late.
The wild goose flies after the sun;
My tree it does not perch upon.
The letter's put in the cask there;
Bugs and moths do it eat and tear.
This letter I'd to the stream throw;
It may reach someone with the flow.
If one opens it, I don't care,
It may cause a trouble somewhere.

* on the cloth I write: A letter to a very important person was usually written on cloth in ancient China, as is recorded in *The Book of the Latter Han*.
* wild goose: an undomesticated goose that is caring and responsible, taken as a symbol of benevolence, righteousness, good manner, wisdom, and faith in Chinese culture.

其　四

芙蓉娇绿波，
桃李夸白日。
偶蒙春风荣，
生此艳阳质。
岂无佳人色？
但恐花不实。
宛转龙火飞，
零落互相失。
讵知凌寒松，
千载长守一？

No. 4

The lotus with her green does blink;
The peach to the sun shows her pink.
So caressed by spring and its balm,
They grow with brilliance and charm.
How can she have no colors fair?
I'm afraid, no fruit she can bear.
Once the majesty does off fly,
How lonely, where can she rely?
Don't you see the pine in clouds cold
For e'er stand and the One uphold?

---

* peach: any of the plant (*Prunus Percica*), bearing a fleshy, juicy, edible drupe, cultivated in many varieties in temperate zones considered sacred in China, often used as a metaphor for a young woman, as a section of a poem in *The Book of Songs* reads: "The peach twigs sway, / Ablaze the flower; / Now she's married away, / Befitting her new bower."

* the One: a philosophical concept of Wordism, the beginning of all things, as is defined in *Sir Lush*, "In the beginning was the None, having nothing, having no name. Then there arose the One, and nothing was formed yet." Similarly, in the West, God is the One, Self-subsisting Reality. The One in the West and the One in the East are actually one, identifiable though in different languages.

其 五

十五游神仙，
仙游未曾歇。
吹笙坐松风，
泛瑟窥海月。
西山玉童子，
使我炼金骨。
欲逐黄鹤飞，
相呼向蓬阙。

No. 5

At fifteen, immortal I'd be;
Tours for the Word do allure me.
I sit in a pine sough to flute,
And gaze at the sea moon to lute.
The fairy child atop Mt. West
Does temper my bones to the best.
I'd chase the yellow crane that flies
To Fairyland, to Paradise.

* the Word: referring to Tao if transliterated, the most significant and profoundest concept in Chinese philosophy. The Word has progenitive power and is the creator of all things. According to Laocius's *The Word and the World*: "The Word is void, but its use is infinite. O deep! It seems to be the root of all things."
* Mt. West: the Western Mountains, borrowed from Tsao P'i, that is, Lord Civil of Way's verse: How high the western mountains stand. / Stand, stand they; you can see no brink. / Above there loom two fairies grand; / They eat nothing, nothing they drink.
* crane: one of a family of large, long-necked, long-legged, heronlike birds allied to the

rails, a symbol of integrity and longevity in Chinese culture, only second to the phoenix in cultural importance.
* Fairyland: an ideal abode for immortals, sometimes thought of as being in the middle of East Sea, sometimes in the sky, the same as Paradise or Shangrila.

其 六

西国有美女,
结楼青云端。
蛾眉艳晓月,
一笑倾城欢。
高节不可夺,
炯心如凝丹。
常恐彩色晚,
不为人所观。
安得配君子,
共乘双飞鸾。

No. 6

There's a belle in the country west;
Her tower is high, by clouds caressed.
The moon's lured by her brows or frown;
Her smile does beguile the whole town.
With her grace no one can compare;
Her heart's staunch like cinnabar rare.
But all riots of blossoms will fade,
No longer well liked, I'm afraid.
A faithful man may you come by,
So like phoenixes you could fly.

---

* Her heart's staunch like cinnabar rare: allusion to the words of Hua Chang (A.D. 232 - A.D. 300), a litterateur in the Chin dynasty. He once said to his emperor: "I, an old subject of our former emperor, have a heart like cinnabar." Cinnabar is a crystallized red mercuric sulfide, HgS, the chief ore of mercury, the raw mineral material for

elixir in Wordist alchemy.
* Phoenix: In Chinese myths, phoenixes, auspicious birds, unlike ordinary ones, only perch on parasol trees, and only eat bamboo shoots and pearly stone.

其 七

竭来荆山客，
谁为珉玉分？
良宝绝见弃，
虚持三献君。
直木忌先伐，
芬兰哀自焚。
盈满天所损，
沉冥道所群。
东海有碧水，
西山多白云。
鲁连及夷齐，
可以蹑清芬。

No. 7

You come from Mt. Chaste with your jade;
None knows your value, I'm afraid.
Your treasured jade they all disdain,
Presented to the Lord in vain.
To be felled a straight tree is prone;
The orchid burned is grieved alone.
Isn't what's full by Heaven spilled?
Isn't what's void by the Word filled?
East Sea holds lots of water clear;
West hills see many clouds appear.
These two are where saints used to dwell;
There I'll get vim and balm as well.

* Mt. Chaste: a mountain in today's Hupei Province, located on the west bank of the River Han. It's said to be the mountain where Ho Pien found the jade. Ho Pien presented the crude jade stone he found to monarchs of Ch'u but failed twice. Ho held the jade stone crying bitterly for the previous misjudgment. Up to this point, the precious jade was finally appreciated by the new lord.
* orchid: a terrestrial or epiphytic monocotyledonous plant having thickened bulbous roots and often very showy distinctive flowers, one of the four most important floral images in Chinese literature, which are wintersweet, orchid, bamboo and chrysanthemum.
* the Word: referring to Tao if transliterated, the most significant and profoundest concept in Chinese philosophy. The Word is fully elucidated in *The Word and the World*, the single book that Laocius wrote all his wisdom into. Its importance can be seen in this verse:"The Word is void, but its use is infinite. O deep! It seems to be the root of all things."
* East Sea: what is now East China Sea, with an area of 770 thousand square kilometers.

其 八

嘉谷隐丰草，
草深苗且稀。
农夫既不异，
孤穗将安归。
常恐委畴陇，
忽与秋蓬飞。
乌得荐宗庙，
为君生光辉。

No. 8

Wild weeds will fine crops subdue;
The weeds are deep, and crops are few.
If good from bad farmers can't tell,
Then where can the lonely ears dwell?
I may fall mid tombs I oft frown
And then fly up with thistledown.
May you offer me to the shrine
So that with you I could there shine.

* thistledown: the pappus of a thistle, a kind of vigorous prickly plant with cylindrical or globular heads of tubular purple flowers, an important image in Chinese Literature, a symbol of helpless vagrancy or straying.

寓言三首
Three Fables

其 一

周公负斧扆,
成王何夔夔?
武王昔不豫,
剪爪投河湄。
贤圣遇谗慝,
不免人君疑。
天风拔大木,
禾黍咸伤萎。
管蔡扇苍蝇,
公赋鸱鸮诗。
金縢若不启,
忠信谁明之。

No. 1

Prince of Chough, loved, stood by the screen;
King Complete so wary had been!
When King Martial was grabbed with rue,
The Prince his clipped nails downstream threw.
All sages have spites in and out;
E'en a king may incur a doubt.
A high wind may topple a tree;
All crops fall down and destroyed be.
Kuan and Ts'ai rose like green head flies;

The Prince wrote *Owls* to them chastise.

If unopened had been Gold Cask,

Who's faithful and true, you might ask.

* Prince of Chough: Prince of Chough (cir. 1100 B.C.-?), referring to the brother of King Martial of Chough (? - 1043 B.C.). He acted as a regent when King Complete was too young to govern the country and gave the power back to the king when the latter was able to manage the government.
* screen: a curtain which separates or cuts off, shelters or protects as a light partition, a common image in Chinese literature. A poem in *The Book of Songs* reads like this: "You wait for me before the screen; / Your hat-rings white do tinkle clean, / And your rubies brilliantly sheen."
* King Complete: King Complete (1055 B.C.- 1021 B.C.), the second king of Chough and the son of King Martial of Chough (? - 1043 B.C.).
* King Martial: King Martial(? - 1043 B.C.), the Founder of Chough, the second son of King Civil (1152 B.C.- 1056 B.C.). He inherited the throne when King Civil died in 1050 B.C.
* Kuan and Ts'ai: King Civil's 3rd and 5th son. Dissatisfied with the regency, suspecting that it was detrimental to the young king, they coerced Wukeng (? - cir. 1118 B.C.), a son of King Chow of Yin's, into rebellion. Prince of Chough, taking the order from the king, suppressed the rebellion, killed Kuan and sent Ts'ai into exile.
* *Owls*: a poem composed by Prince of Chough, which reads like this: Hateful owl, hateful owl, My kids you've taken all, / Do not destroy my hall. / Both diligent and ware, / I've raised my kids with care.
* Gold Cask: Prince of Chough once wrote a letter to demonstrate his devotion to King Martial, and the letter was kept in a gold cask. When King Complete grew up, he misunderstood Prince of Chough until he read the the letter in the gold cask.

其 二

遥裔双彩凤，
婉娈三青禽。
往还瑶台里，
鸣舞玉山岑。
以欢秦蛾意，
复得王母心。
区区精卫鸟，
衔木空哀吟。

No. 2

The two phoenixes skywards dance;
The three messengers sprucely prance.
They shuttle to and from Jade Mound
And on Mt. Jade high praises sound.
They can please Fair Ch'in with their art,
And again win Queen Mother's heart.
Jayway who holds twigs in her beak,
So despised, in vain does there shriek.

* Phoenix: In Chinese myths, phoenixes, auspicious birds, unlike ordinary ones, only perch on parasol trees, and only eat bamboo shoots and pearly stone.
* Jade Mound: one of the twelve jade mounds on Mt. Queen, each a thousand feet wide with five colors of jade as their base.
* Mt. Jade: referring to Mt. Queen, or Mt. Kunlun if transliterated, the most sacred mountain in China. It starts from the Eastern Pamir Plateau, stretches across New Land (Hsinchiang) and Tibet, and extends to Ch'inghai, with an average altitude of 5,500 – 6,000 meters. In Chinese myths, Mt. Queen is where Mother West dwells.
* Fair Ch'in: referring to the daughter of Lord Solemn of Ch'in (? – 621 B.C.), who

was good at playing the flute. Once in her dream, she dreamed of a young man riding a phoenix to play music with her. So Lord Solemn found the young man and married his daughter to him.
* Queen Mother: referring to Mother West, a sovereign goddess living on Mt. Queen in Chinese myths. She was originally described as human-bodied, tiger-toothed, leopard-tailed and hoopoe-haired, regarded as a goddess in charge of women protection, marriage and procreation, and longevity.
* Jayway: According to legend, a daughter of Magic Farmer was drowned in East Sea and turned into a bird named Jayway. It looks like a crow or jay, but with an annular head, a white beak, and red feet, used to carrying stone and wood in an attempt to fill up the sea.

其 三

长安春色归，
先入青门道。
绿杨不自持，
从风欲倾倒。
海燕还秦宫，
双飞入帘栊。
相思不相见，
托梦辽城东。

No. 3

Spring comes back to Capital Town,
Thru Bluegate and all the way down.
The willow can't stand well at all;
In the wind it is prone to fall.
The petrels back to Ch'in House fly,
Both thru the curtain bars so high.
I can't see you as you're so far!
I'll send my dream to where you are.

* the Bluegate: referring to the east gate of Long Peace, where Shao P'ing, Lord Eastridge in the Ch'in dynasty, used to grow melons after demotion.
* petrel: a member of any of three families of small marine tubenose birds with long wings, including storm petrels, and shearwaters.

秋 夕 旅 怀

凉风度秋海，
吹我乡思飞。
连山去无际，
流水何时归。
目极浮云色，
心断明月晖。
芳草歇柔艳，
白露催寒衣。
梦长银汉落，
觉罢天星稀。
含悲想旧国，
泣下谁能挥。

Touched While Travelling at Dusk in Autumn

Autumn wind blows to the sea chill
And blows my woe to my home town.
So vast it wends hill upon hill;
Will the river flow back, here down?
I look afar at the clouds dark,
Disheartened at the moon's cold hue.
The grass no longer rank but stark,
"Winter clothes", I'm urged by white dew.
I dream of the Milky Way's fall
And wake to find stars very few.

I sigh, and my land I recall;
Who can check my tears? Sad, they flow.

* the Milky Way: the Silver River in Chinese mythology, the river in the sky, which was made by Queen Mother with her hair pin; a luminous band circling the heavens composed of stars and nebulae; the Galaxy.

感 遇 四 首

Touched, Four Poems

其 一

吾爱王子晋，
得道伊洛滨。
金骨既不毁，
玉颜长自春。
可怜浮丘公，
猗靡与情亲。
举首白日间，
分明谢时人。
二仙去已远，
梦想空殷勤。

No. 1

Prince of Front I love very much;
He by the Lo attained the Word.
His bones remain like gold as such
And his face was in prime restored.
Floating Knoll was also adored,
With whom we could all well accord.
We share the light of the same day,
But in different worlds we now stay.
The two immortals far off gone,
Here, only my dream lingers on.

* Prince of Front: Prince of Front (567 B.C.- 549 B.C.), the first son of King Spirit of Chough (795 B.C.- 771 B.C.). He was an intelligent and courageous young man. Though high as a prince, he had few desires and was keen on the Word. As legend goes, he met Master Floating Knoll at the Lo River, followed him to deep mountains, and he died young, he rose to the sky, riding a white crane, and became immortal.
* the Lo: the Lo River, which flows through the ancient capital Loshine.
* the Word: referring to Tao if transliterated, the most significant and profoundest concept in Chinese philosophy. The Word is identifiable with the Word or Logos in the West, as there is an enormous amount of common ground in the two cosmologies and the doctrines concerning the most fundamental matters such as "the Word is the One" and "God is the One", and the personalization of Being, the progenitor of finite spirits, which are subordinate kinds of Being or merely appearances of the Divine, the One.
* Floating Knoll: a legendary immortal.

其 二

可叹东篱菊，
茎疏叶且微。
虽言异兰蕙，
亦自有芳菲。
未泛盈樽酒，
徒沾清露辉。
当荣君不采，
飘落欲何依。

No. 2

By East Hedge chrysanthemum be,
Its stalk and leaves are thin and wee.
Orchids and lilies different smell;
Each has its charm and balm as well.
I have never drunk Lord Glee's wine,
My clothes touched with his dewy shine.
The blooms you should pick while you may;
All too soon, they will fade away.

* East Hedge: When Poolbright T'ao (A.D. 352 – A.D. 427) lived in seclusion, he used to plant chrysanthemums by his east hedge.
* Lord Glee: the court title of Lingyün Hsieh (A.D. 385 – A.D. 433), a highborn poet, general, Buddhist, idyllist, and traveler, especially famous for his landscape poems.
* orchid: any of a widely distributed family of terrestrial or epiphytic monocotyledonous plants having thickened bulbous roots and often very showy distinctive flowers, one of the four most important floral images in Chinese literature, which are wintersweet, orchid, bamboo and chrysanthemum.

其 三

昔余闻姮娥，
窃药驻云发。
不自娇玉颜，
方希炼金骨。
飞去身莫返，
含笑坐明月。
紫宫夸蛾眉，
随手会凋歇。

No. 3

I hear once E'rfair, a girl fair,
Stole a cure-all for her black hair.
Her glamour she did not cherish,
But hoped her bones would not perish.
Then she flew away all too soon;
Now she sits, smiling, on the moon.
Beauties in the palace, don't brag!
Every while your glamor may sag.

* E'rfair: the goddess living on the moon. She was the wife of King Archer, who shot nine suns off the sky according to legend. It is said that she flew to the moon and lived away from her husband because she stole elixir from Queen Mother.
* the moon: the celestial body that revolves around the earth from west to east as a satellite, which appears at night and gives off shining silvery light, an image of purity and solitude in Chinese culture.

其 四

宋玉事楚王，
立身本高洁。
巫山赋彩云，
郢路歌白雪。
举国莫能和，
巴人皆卷舌。
一感登徒言，
恩情遂中绝。

No. 4

Then Jade Sung did serve King of Ch'u;
He stood erect, so staunch and true.
At Mt. Witch he sang of clouds bright;
In Mid-Ying he well praised snow white.
To match him, the state had no one,
And the Pa folks withdrew their tongue.
Tengt'u's slander the lord believed;
Sung lost as the king was deceived.

* Jade Sung: Jade Sung (cir. 298 B.C.- cir. 222 B.C.), a student of Yüan Ch'ü's, and a famous poet in the Warring States period. He, one of the four most handsome men in ancient China, once served as an official for King Hsiang of Ch'u (? - 263 B.C.).
* Mt. Witch: a mythical and religious mountain, which was thought to be a range of mountains in Sha'anhsi.
* Mid-Ying: referring to the capital of Ch'u.
* the Pa folks: the folks from the State of Pa, usually regarded as countrified ones.
* Tengt'u: a figure in Jade Sung's verse.

翰林读书言怀呈集贤诸学士

晨趋紫禁中，
夕待金门诏。
观书散遗帙，
探古穷至妙。
片言苟会心，
掩卷忽而笑。
青蝇易相点，
白雪难同调。
本是疏散人，
屡贻褊促诮。
云天属清朗，
林壑忆游眺。
或时清风来，
闲倚栏下啸。
严光桐庐溪，
谢客临海峤。
功成谢人间，
从此一投钓。

Expressing My Will to the Scholars When Reading in Brushwood

The morn sees me levee await;
The dusk sees me wait at Gold Gate.
I read books passed on from before,
And profundities I explore.

If I find something like my style,
I'll close the book for a sweet smile.
Green head flies rush to the same lay;
Sunny Spring or *Snow White* few can play.
Lazy-sloppy I used to be;
Flunkies, funnies, they jeer at me.
High is the sky and crisp the air;
Once to the valleys I did stare.
Sometimes a soothing breeze blows by;
Leaning on the rail, long I cry.
Yan angled in the T'unglu Stream;
Hsieh did in the far-off sea swim.
When can I from the world retire
And go fishing for a life higher?

* levee: a morning reception or an assembly at the court of a sovereign or at the house of a great personage. In ancient China, a levee at court was held every five days.
* Gold Gate: implying an imperial academy. Courtiers and officials would wait here before the court was opened.
* *Sunny Spring* or *Snow White*: ancient songs representing sophisticated arts.
* Yan: referring to Tsuling Yan (39 B.C.- A.D. 41), a renowned hermit in the Han dynasty. He showed his talent at an early age. After Hsiu Liu was enthroned to be the emperor of Eastern Han, Yan was invited several times to serve the court. Though the emperor was an acquaintance of his, Yan declined the offer and chose to live in seclusion in the Richspring Hills.
* T'unglu: a place where Tsuling Yan used to stay free from the worldly troubles.
* Hsieh: referring to Lingyün Hsieh (A.D. 385 - A.D. 433), a highborn poet, idyllist, Buddhist and traveler in the Southern and Northern Dynasties, famous for his landscape poems.

寻阳紫极宫感秋作

何处闻秋声,
翛翛北窗竹。
回薄万古心,
揽之不盈掬。
静坐观众妙,
浩然媚幽独。
白云南山来,
就我檐下宿。
懒从唐生决,
羞访季主卜。
四十九年非,
一往不可复。
野情转萧洒,
世道有翻覆。
陶令归去来,
田家酒应熟。

Touched at the Autumn View at Purple Palace in Bankshine

Where is the autumn from, as soughs?
By the window, the bamboo bows.
Old tales go back to the old land;
I have a few, not filled my hand.
Sitting, so calm, nuances I see;
Seated, so quiet, I feel care-free.

White clouds come from the southern hills

They will sleep twixt my eaves and sills.

I won't seek T'ang to decide well;

I won't ask Chi who does foretell.

It's forty nine years to a day;

What is gone can no longer stay.

Wild romance may turn out a crown;

The way of life may turn up and down.

Away Lord Glee from here has gone;

The farmer's wine's ready, come on.

* Purple Palace: a Wordist temple.
* Bankshine: an ancient name of present-day Chiuchiang, Chianghsi Province.
* T'ang: referring to Chü T'ang, a physiognomist in the Warring States period.
* Chi: referring to Chichu Ssuma, a representative Wordist in the Han dynasty.
* Lord Glee: the court title of Lingyün Hsieh (A.D. 385 – A.D. 433), a highborn poet, Buddhist, idyllist and traveler, especially famous for his landscape poems.

江上秋怀

餐霞卧旧壑,
散发谢远游。
山蝉号枯桑,
始复知天秋。
朔雁别海裔,
越燕辞江楼。
飒飒风卷沙,
茫茫雾萦洲。
黄云结暮色,
白水扬寒流。
恻怆心自悲,
潺湲泪难收。
蘅兰方萧瑟,
长叹令人愁。

An Impromptu of Autumn on the River

Back to the dale I'll eat clouds fair,
Lying there with my untied hair.
Cicadas to dried mulberries shrill,
And I know there comes autumn chill.
The wild geese take leave of the shore;
The swallows from the tower there soar.
The autumn sough whirls up the sand;
The haze to the shoal does expand.
The yellow clouds in the dusk swell;

The white water bumps the cold spell.
In my heart gushes up my woe;
Gurgling, my tears ceaselessly flow.
Lilies and orchids will soon dry;
At this sad scene, long, long I sigh.

* eat clouds: eating clouds is one way of cultivating vital energy in Wordist practice.
* cicada: a homopterous insect that sings its song of summer and shrills in autumn, a symbol of death and resurrection in Chinese culture because of its metamorphosis and recycle. Therefore, in ancient China, a jade cicada figure was put in the mouth of a dead body with such an intention of eternal life.
* wild goose: an undomesticated goose that is caring and responsible, taken as a symbol of benevolence, righteousness, good manner, wisdom, and faith in Chinese culture.
* swallow: a passerine black bird, with short broad, depressed bill, long pointed wings, and forked tail, noted for fleeting flight and migratory habits. In Chinese culture, swallows are welcome to live with a family with their nest on a beam.
* orchid: a monocotyledonous plant having thickened bulbous roots and often very showy distinctive flowers, one of the four most important floral images in Chinese literature, which are wintersweet, orchid, bamboo and chrysanthemum.

秋夕书怀

北风吹海雁，
南渡落寒声。
感此潇湘客，
凄其流浪情。
海怀结沧洲，
霞想游赤城。
始探蓬壶事，
旋觉天地轻。
澹然吟高秋，
闲卧瞻太清。
萝月掩空幕，
松霜结前楹。
灭见息群动，
猎微穷至精。
桃花有源水，
可以保吾生。

Expressing Myself at Dusk in Autumn

The northern wind blows wild geese chill;
They fly south and in coldness shrill.
A vagrant, I drift in South Clime,
My heart with the wild geese does chime.
I'd tour seas and isles up and down
Or like a cloud visit Red Town.
Fleabane Pot I start to explore,

Heaven and earth felt light, e'er more.
I sing to the brisk autumn breeze
And think Pure Court lying at ease.
The moon above beams to the vines;
The frost upon the columns shines.
In void all things merge with the One,
So subtly made, so subtly done.
Peach Blossoms sees the stream so clean;
Here, I'd be well as they have been.

* wild goose: an undomesticated goose that is caring and responsible, taken as a symbol of benevolence, righteousness, good manner, wisdom, and faith in Chinese culture.
* South Clime: referring to the Hsiang land, approximately today's Hunan Province.
* Red Town: referring to Mt. Red Town, one kilometer from today's Heaven Mound (Tient'ai) County, Chechiang Province.
* Fleabane Pot: a legendary fairy isle on East Sea, also known as P'englai Isle or Fairy Ilse.
* Pure Court: a term in Wordism indicating the realm of real freedom.
* the One: a philosophical concept of Wordism, the beginning of all things, as is defined in *Sir Lush*, "In the beginning was the None, having nothing, having no name. Then there arose the One, and nothing was formed yet." And in Laocius's *The Word and the World*: "The sky has gotten the One, hence blue and clear; the earth has gotten the One, hence staid and still." Similarly, in the West, God is the One, Self-subsisting Reality. The One in the West and the One in the East are actually one, identifiable though in different languages.
* Peach Blossoms: According to Yüanming Tao's writing, a group of Ch'in people fled to Peach Blossom Source to keep away from the turbulent days, and the people and their offsprings had lived and idyllic and isolated life for 500 years before a fisherman of Chin stumbled into the village.

避地司空原言怀

南风昔不竞,
豪圣思经伦。
刘琨与祖逖,
起舞鸡鸣晨。
虽有匡济心,
终为乐祸人。
我则异于是,
潜光皖水滨。
卜筑司空原,
北将天柱邻。
雪霁万里月,
云开九江春。
俟乎太阶平,
然后托微身。
倾家事金鼎,
年貌可长新。
所愿得此道,
终然保清真。
弄景奔日驭,
攀星戏河津。
一随王乔去,
长年玉天宾。

Retiring to Mt. Ssukung

South wind does not stop as of yore;

Saints and sages the world explore.

K'un Liu and Ti Tsu, generals two,

Rose to practice when cocks did crow.

Tho they would strive to save the land,

Framed to fall down, they could not stand.

I've the same fate, a different way;

I could stroll the Wan, a good day.

At last in Ssukung I'd abide,

Three-Sires Temple in the north side.

The moon is brightened by the snow;

The clouds are stroked by a spring blow.

Here I wait for a peaceful day,

So from the court I could well stay.

For elixir I'll spend all gold

So that I'll stay young, never old.

What I wish for is the Great Way,

Wherein keep natural we may.

I would go higher, riding the sun,

And in the Milky Way have fun.

With the Immortal I would fly;

For long Pure Heaven I'd keep by.

* Mt. Ssukung: a mountain in present-day Anhui Province.
* K'un Liu: K'un Liu (A.D. 271 - A.D. 318), a statesman, litterateur, musician and military strategist in the Chin dynasty.
* Ti Tsu: Ti Tsu (A.D. 266 - A.D. 321), a military strategist in the Chin dynasty. Ti Tsu and K'un Liu were friends. One night, Tsu heard a crowing, and he woke Liu, inviting him to practice sword skill at dawn.
* the Wan: the Wan River, a branch of the Long River, also known as the Back River.
* Ssukung: referring to Ssukung Pool half way to the top of Mt. Ssukung, 80 kilometers northwest from Great Lake (T'aihu).
* Three-Sires Temple: a Buddhist temple on Mt. Heaven Column, Anhui.

* the Great Way: referring to the Word.
* the Milky Way: the Silver River in Chinese mythology; a luminous band circling the heavens composed of stars and nebulae; the Galaxy.
* the Immortal: referring to Prince of Front (567 B.C.-549 B.C.), the first son of King Spirit of Chough. He was an intelligent and courageous young man. Though high as a prince, he had few desires and was keen on the Word. As legend goes, he met Mister Floating Knoll at the Lo River, followed him to deep mountains, and after his early death he rose to the sky, riding a white crane, and became an immortal.
* Pure Heaven: a heavenly abode pure like jade as is believed by Wordists.

上崔相百忧章（时在浔阳狱）

共工赫怒，
天维中摧。
鲲鲸喷荡，
扬涛起雷。
鱼龙陷人，
成此祸胎。
火焚昆山，
玉石相磓。
仰希霖雨，
洒宝炎煨。
箭发石开，
戈挥日回。
邹衍恸哭，
燕霜飒来。
微诚不感，
犹絷夏台。
苍鹰搏攫，
丹棘崔嵬。
豪圣凋枯，
王风伤哀。
斯文未丧，
东岳岂颓。
穆逃楚难，
邹脱吴灾。
见机苦迟，
二公所咍。
骥不骤进，

麟何来哉！
星离一门，
草掷二孩。
万愤结习，
忧从中催。
金瑟玉壶，
尽为愁媒。
举酒太息，
泣血盈杯。
台星再朗，
天网重恢。
屈法申恩，
弃瑕取材。
冶长非罪，
尼父无猜。
覆盆傥举，
应照寒灰。

Writing to Premier Ts'ui to Vent My Rues (Jailed in Bankshine)

Cowork into rage flies
And will o'erturn the skies.
There spurts water the whale
And lifts a thundering hail.
The courtiers frame and press,
Hence all suffer the distress.
Mt. Queen is ablaze, burned;
Jade and stone are o'erturned.
Now I pray for a rain

To put out the fire main.
An arrow breaks the stone;
A spear's to the sun thrown.
Yan Tsou, wronged, sadly cries;
Yan's Land in hoarfrost lies.
My efforts have all failed;
In Summer Mound I'm jailed.
The warders like hawks call,
Thorns planted on the wall.
Even saints like flowers die,
And at *Airs* all will sigh.
But time will still elapse;
Mt. East will ne'er collapse.
Sheng Mu's managed to flee;
Tsou escaped from Wu to be free.
But that's not happened here;
The two will at me sneer.
A swift horse won't here run;
Unicorns will me shun.
The family's deranged,
Two kids not well arranged.
Anger bursts from my chest;
I'm worried and distressed.
For all lute tunes and wine,
I feel painful and whine.
I sigh, holding my cup,
With blood and tears turned up.
The stars shine and high be!
Will you please pardon me?
May you forgive what's gone,
Not minding what I've done.

> Kungyeh was freed of guilt,
> Confucius' trust well built.
> The o'erturned pot turned right,
> Once ash, I now shine bright.

* Cowork: God of Water in Chinese mythology. Cowork had a fight with Jade Crown (Chuanhsu), and he broke a sky pillar out of rage.
* whale: a giant cetaceous mammal of fish-like form, especially one of the large pelagic species, as distinguished from dolphins and porpoises.
* Mt. Queen: or Mt. Kunlun if transliterated, the most sacred mountain in China. It starts from the Eastern Pamir Plateau, stretches across New Land (Hsinchiang) and Tibet, and extends to Ch'inghai, with an average altitude of 5,500 – 6,000 meters. In Chinese myths, Mt. Queen is where Mother West dwells.
* Yan Tsou: Yan Tsou (324 B.C.- 250 B.C.), a representative scholar of Wordism and the founder of Five Elements Theory. Tsou suffered from false imprisonment for his lord, King of Yan, believed in slander against Tsou. The false imprisonment caused a blast of hoarfrost in June.
* Summer Mound: a prison. According to *Historical Records*, Stump, the first king of Hsia, jailed Hotspring, the fist king of Shang here.
* Sheng Mu: a man from Lu in the Han dynasty. Mu was treated by King of Ch'u with great courtesy. When they met, King of Ch'u usually prepared wine for Mu. After the new lord's enthronement, the new crown did not prepare wine and Mu knew it was time to leave.
* Tsou: referring to Tsou Yang, a litterateur with high reputation in the Western Han dynasty. He once served King of Wu, but after several failures in admonishing the lord, Tsou Yang left Wu.
* Wu: referring to Eastern Wu founded by Ch'üan Sun.
* unicorn: a fabulous deer-like animal with one horn, a symbol of saintliness and divinity in Chinese culture. Confucius lamented the death of a unicorn captured and hence stopped compiling *The Spring and Autumn Annals* and died before long.
* Kungyeh: Kungyeh (519 B.C.- 470 B.C.), a student of Confucius's. He was put into prison though innocent. Confucius knew it was false imprisonment, so he married his daughter to Kungyeh.
* Confucius: Confucius (551 B.C.- 479 B.C.), a renowned thinker, educator and statesman in the Spring and Autumn period, born in the State of Lu, who was the founder of Confucianism and who has had exerted profound influence on Chinese culture.

万愤词投魏郎中

海水渤潏，
人罹鲸鲵。
何六龙之浩荡，
迁白日于秦西。
九土星分，
嗷嗷凄凄。
南冠君子，
呼天而啼。
恋高堂而掩泣，
泪血地而成泥。
狱户春而不草，
独幽怨而沈迷。
兄九江兮弟三峡，
悲羽化之难齐。
穆陵关北愁爱子，
豫章天南隔老妻。
一门骨肉散百草，
遇难不复相提携。
树榛拔桂，
囚鸾宠鸡。
舜昔授禹，
伯成耕犁。
德自此衰，
吾将安栖。
好我者恤我，
不好我者何忍临危而相挤。
子胥鸱夷，

彭越醢醢。
自古豪烈，
胡为此繁？
苍苍之天，
高乎视低。
如其听卑，
脱我牢狴。
倪辨美玉，
君收白珪。

To Way, the Royal Guard, to Vent My Anger

The torrents loudly wail,
Folks devoured by the whale.
How grand the royals, horses and carts!
E'en the white sun west from Ch'in departs.
The Nine Realms falling down,
Refugees' cries there drown.
Like Ee Chung, atop, on high,
I, jailed, shout to the sky.
O parents, I miss you, tear and blood,
Tear and blood drop, running into mud.
Spring's come, but by the jail no grass grows;
Alone, I'm listless, drowned in my woes.
My bros in the Nine and Three Gorges, why,
We couldn't meet; I've no wings to fly.
I miss my children north of Sternridge Pass,
South there, my wife's kept off from me, alas
My family is like grasses dispersed;

We can't help each other, by chaos cursed.

Laurels felled, hazels grow;

Phoenix jailed, roosters crow.

Hibiscus gave Worm throne

Tsukao did farm alone.

Virtues decrease from now;

Where can I rest, and how?

Those who love me are concerned;

Those who don't, when I'm in trouble, will have me spurned.

Wu was drowned in a sac;

P'eng was chopped up, alack.

All gallants, high and great,

Why heave up such a state?

O great sky, o vast sky,

You o'erlook us on high!

Can you now hear my wail?

Pray free me from the jail.

Good from bad if you'd tell,

Take this jade from the dell.

* Ch'in: the State of Ch'in (905 B.C.– 206 B.C.), one of the most powerful vassal states in the Chough dynasty, which developed into the first unified regime of China, i.e. the Ch'in Empire.
* the Nine Realms: an alternative name for China, which was divided into nine realms by Worm, the first king of Hsia.
* Ee Chung: a man from Ch'u who kept wearing Ch'u's hat though captured by Chin.
* the Nine: referring to Bankshine, also known as the Nine Rivers, now a city of present-day Chianghsi Province.
* Three Gorges: referring to the three gorges of the Yangtze River, including Big Pond Gorge, Witch Gorge, and Westridge Gorge. It implies the area around the three gorges.
* Sternridge Pass: located in Shantung.
* laurel: an evergreen shrub with aromatic, lance-shaped leaves, yellowish flowers, and

succulent, cherry-like fruit.
* hazel: a bushy shrub or small tree of the birch family (genus *Corylus*) yielding a hard-shelled edible nut enclosed in a leafy involucre.
* Hibiscus: Shun if transliterated, the Double-pupiled One, an ancient sovereign, a descendant of Lord Yellow, regarded as one of Five Lords in prehistoric China.
* Worm: the founding lord of Hsia, who took over the leadership from Hibiscus. It was said that Mound was put in jail, having lost his morality, and Hibiscus died in a moor when he was in a tour. The poet borrowed the ancient legend to imply that the reign of T'ang was in danger of being destroyed.
* Tsukao: a lord in Mound's reign. He resigned from post and farmed on his land after Hibiscus gave his throne to Worm as Tsukao believed that there would be a mess.
* Wu: referring to Tsehsu Wu (559 B.C.- 484 B.C.), a senior official of Wu. At his old age, his suggestion was denied and he was alienated by the king. King of Wu was irritated by the latter's complaints, so he gave him a sword to commit suicide. After his death, the king put his body in a leather bag and threw it into a river.
* P'eng: referring to Yüeh P'eng (? - A.D. 196), one of the three best generals of early Han (the other two being Hsin Han and Pu Ying), a founding commander of the Han Empire, who was killed for a possibility of treason.

荆州贼平临洞庭言怀作

修蛇横洞庭，
吞象临江岛。
积骨成巴陵，
遗言闻楚老。
水穷三苗国，
地窄三湘道。
岁晏天峥嵘，
时危人枯槁。
思归阴丧乱，
去国伤怀抱。
郢路方丘墟，
章华亦倾倒。
风悲猿啸苦，
木落鸿飞早。
日隐西赤沙，
月明东城草。
关河望已绝，
氛雾行当扫。
长叫天可闻，
吾将问苍昊。

Expressing My Anger at Cavehall When Rebels Are Wiped Out in Chaste

By Lake Cavehall a huge serpent
Devoured the isle-side elephant.

Its bones made a pile, the Pa Hill.
A Ch'u man tells me of the kill.
The Three Sprouts by water abide;
The Three Hsiangs till e'en on roadside.
Hard life sees the end of the year;
Hard times make all old and all drear.
All have been disturbed by the war;
I leave my land, so filled with sore.
Ying's boulevards and knolls lie waste;
The palace is fallen, debased.
The wind does sigh and monkeys cry;
The leaves sway dry and wild geese fly.
The sun sets west to the sand red;
The moon shines east to town grass spread.
To the mountain and pass I gaze;
We should sweep off all wicked haze.
I cry, and can you hear my cry?
I raise my head to ask the sky.

* Chaste: Chingchow if transliterated, an old town on the Long River or a geographical region including areas of present-day Hupei and Hunan provinces.
* Lake Cavehall: a lake in today's Hunan Province, rich with natural and cultural resources.
* elephant: a massively built, almost hairless ungulate mammal of Asia and Africa, the largest of existing land animals, having a flexible proboscis or trunk, and the upper incisors developed as tusks valued as the chief source of ivory.
* the Pa Hill: referring to Hillshine, located south of Mt. Mufu and near Lake Cavehall, first built in 505 B.C. in present-day Yüehyang, Hunan Province.
* Sprouts: Three Sprouts, an ethnic minority living in the southwest of China. A geographical region including areas of present-day Hupei and Hunan provinces. Some Sprouts live in other Asian coungtries.
* Three Hsiangs: referring to present-day Hunan Province. The Hsiang River flows into three rivers, the Li, the Cheng and the Hsiao, hence the name Three Hsiangs.

* Ying: the capital of Ch'u in the Chough dynasty, near present-day Chaston (Chingchow), Hupei Province.
* wild goose: an undomesticated goose that is caring and responsible, taken as a symbol of benevolence, righteousness, good manner, wisdom, and faith in Chinese culture.

览 镜 书 怀

得道无古今，
失道还衰老。
自笑镜中人，
白发如霜草。
扪心空叹息，
问影何枯槁？
桃李竟何言，
终成南山皓。

An Impromptu When Looking into a Mirror

One can gain the Word now as past;
Once the Word's lost, he ages fast.
I laugh into the mirror, where
Like frosted grass is my white hair.
Pommeling my chest, I long sigh:
Why do you look so gaunt, o why?
Peach and plum need nothing to say;
I'll join Four Gray Heads with hair gray.

* the Word: referring to Tao if transliterated, the most significant and profoundest concept in Chinese philosophy.
* According to Laocius's *The Word and the World*: "The Word is void, but its use is infinite. O deep! It seems to be the root of all things."
* Four Gray Heads: referring to the four old Wordists living at Mt. Shang, their hermitage since they fled the tyranny of Emperor First of Ch'in. They withdrew from the world toward the close of the reappeared upon the establishment of the Han dynasty and were welcomed and venerated by the new emperor.

田 园 言 怀

贾谊三年谪，
班超万里侯。
何如牵白犊，
饮水对清流。

On a Farmland

Ee Chia was in exile three years;
Ch'ao Pan did take pains to join peers.
Could they match him with a calf white,
Which drinks the current clearly bright.

* Ee Chia: Ee Chia (200 B.C.- 168 B.C.), a political commentator and litterateur, who gained his fame when he was young. When he served as an official, he was envied by those higher-ranking ministers. In 176 B.C., Chia was exiled to Long Sand.
* Ch'ao Pan: Ch'ao Pan (A.D. 32 - A.D. 102), a renowned military strategist and diplomat in the Eastern Han dynasty. Ch'ao made great achievements in thirty-one years' pacification in the western regions.

江 南 春 怀

青春几何时，
黄鸟鸣不歇。
天涯失乡路，
江外老华发。
心飞秦塞云，
影滞楚关月。
身世殊烂漫，
田园久芜没。
岁晏何所从？
长歌谢金阙。

A Spring Impromptu in the South

How long will the spring last, how long?
The orioles their song do prolong.
I'm lost! Where is my hometown, where?
Drifting around, I've grown gray hair.
To clouds o'er Ch'in Pass, my heart flies,
My shade kept by the moonlit skies.
I should have had a future bright,
But my farmland is drear, in plight.
Where shall I go now ends the year?
I sing good-bye to Gold Gate here.

* Ch'in Pass: referring to Case Dale or the land west of Case Dale.
* good-bye to Gold Gate: suggesting the poet's will of retreat from officialdom.

听蜀僧濬弹琴

蜀僧抱绿绮，
西下峨眉峰。
为我一挥手，
如听万壑松。
客心洗流水，
馀响入霜钟。
不觉碧山暮，
秋云暗几重。

Listening to a Monk from Shu Play the Lute

The monk from Shu his green lute brings,
Coming down the west of Mt. Brow.
His deft fingers run thru the strings,
Like pines that in myriad vales sough.
The water washes off all cares;
The strains with a toll ring on high.
The green hills turn dark unawares,
With autumn clouds that dim the sky.

* Shu: one of the earliest kingdoms in China, founded by Silkworm according to legend. In the Three Kingdoms period, a new Shu was established by Pei Liu, hence one of the three kingdoms in that period.
* Mt. Brow: one of the four Buddhist mountains, located in present-day Ssuch'uan Province, named for its elegant brow-shaped silhouette viewed from a distance.

鲁东门观刈蒲

鲁国寒事早，
初霜刈渚蒲。
挥镰若转月，
拂水生连珠。
此草最可珍，
何必贵龙须，
织作玉床席，
欣承清夜娱。
罗衣能再拂，
不畏素尘芜。

Watching Reaping of Cattail to the East of Gate of Lu

The winter comes early to Lu;
She reaps cattail with frosty dew.
She waves a moon-like sickle fast,
Stirring up water beads harassed.
Cattail's like a treasure endeared;
Why should we cherish dragon's beard?
Woven into a bedding mat,
It's cool, for a night cool like that.
Her silk robe could be cleaned again;
She never ever minds a stain!

* cattail: a perennial acquatic plant (genus *Typha*), with long leaves, flowers in

cylindrical terminal spikes, and downy fruit.
* Lu: referring to the State of Lu, a state enfeoffed to Prince of Chough, inherited by his son Firstling Bird, exterminated by Ch'u in 256 B.C.
* dragon's beard: regarded as something precious. As legend goes, a dragon drooped its beard to welcome Jade Emperor to Heaven. His subjects, taking its beards, would like to go with the emperor, but its beard broke half way to Heaven. The broken hair of the beard, left to the world, as is believed, can safeguard families and promote their career.

咏邻女东窗海石榴

鲁女东窗下，
海榴世所稀。
珊瑚映绿水，
未足比光辉。
清香随风发，
落日好鸟归。
愿为东南枝，
低举拂罗衣。
无由共攀折，
引领望金扉。

Ode to the Girl Neighbor by the Sea Pomegranate at Her East Window

By the Lu girl's east window there
Stands a sea pomegranate so rare.
The corals shining in the blue
Cannot compare with its bright hue.
Its balm goes with wind and goes on;
Birds return from the setting sun.
She'd like to be the southeast spray
To sweep dust off her own array.
She can't reach it tho raised her head;
She leers at the window instead.

* sea pomegranate: a kind of pomegranates that originated from east of the sea.
* coral: the hard, stony skeleton secreted by certain marine polyps and often deposited in extensive masses forming reefs and atolls in tropical seas.

南 轩 松

南轩有孤松，
柯叶自绵幂。
清风无闲时，
潇洒终日夕。
阴生古苔绿，
色染秋烟碧。
何当凌云霄，
直上数千尺。

A Pine by South Window

By south window stands a lone pine;
Its lush twigs and leaves sway to shine.
A cool wind may its lithe twigs sway;
How nice and spruce they are all day!
In its shade there appears moss green;
It's all touched with autumn cloud sheen.
When can it grow and grow so high,
Ten thousand feet up to the sky?

* a lone pine: a metaphor for the poet himself, by means of which he expresses his aspiration.
* moss: a tiny, delicate green bryophytic plant growing on damp decaying wood, wet ground, humid rocks or trees, producing capsules which open by an operculum and contain spores. Under a poet's writing brush, it may arouse a poetic feeling or imagination.

咏山樽二首

Ode to the Wooden Cup, Two Poems

其 一

蟠木不雕饰，
且将斤斧疏。
樽成山岳势，
材是栋梁余。
外与金罍并，
中涵玉醴虚。
惭君垂拂拭，
遂忝玳筵居。

No. 1

The crooked wood one need not lop,
Nor need we use axes to chop.
Like a hill the cup made does seem;
As stuff, it is more than a beam.
Now placed beside a golden pot,
It holds nectar to lure a sot.
At your favor I'm shy and pleased;
Please count me for your ornate feast.

---

* nectar: in Chinese and Greek mythologies, the drink of the gods or fairies, hence a metaphor for best wine, that is, wine like nectar, and in botany, the saccharine substance secreted by some plants and forming the base of natural honey.

其 二

拥肿寒山木，
嵌空成酒樽。
愧无江海量，
偃蹇在君门。

No. 2

The wood with warts from the Cold Hill
Is carved as a cup for a fill.
I dare not boast I could drink much;
Before your door, I lounge as such.

* the wood with warts: an allusion to *Sir Lush*, which reads: Then Sir Good told Sir Lush: "I have a giant tree called toon. Its trunk, with lots of warts, can't be gauged; its branches are too twisted to be measured. Standing wayside, it has no carpenter's regard."

初出金门寻王侍御不遇,咏壁上鹦鹉

落羽辞金殿,
孤鸣咤绣衣;
能言终见弃,
还向陇西飞。

Ode to the Parrot on the Wall When I Fail to See Wang, the Royal Servant, Soon After My Being Exiled

Your plumes off, exiled from the hall;
Flapping brocade, alone you call.
You are spurned because you talk much;
Now you fly to West Bulge as such.

* parrot: the bird that can simulate human laughter and speech, having a hooked bill, paired toes, and usually brilliant plumage; a metaphor for the poet himself in this poem.
* West Bulge: Lunghsi if transliterated, name of a shire in the Warring States period and the T'ang dynasty, covering today's Lanchow, West Buldge and Lint'ao.

紫 藤 树

紫藤挂云木，
花蔓宜阳春。
密叶隐歌鸟，
香风留美人。

Wistaria

Wistaria to the tall tree cling;
Its blooms add to the charming spring.
Its dense leaves warblers shade and hide;
Its fragrance lures beauties to bide.

* wistaria: any of a genus of woody twining shrubs of the bean family, with pinnate leaves, elongated pods and handsome clusters of blue, purple, or white flowers.

观放白鹰二首

Watching the White Hawk, Two Poems

其 一

八月边风高，
胡鹰白锦毛。
孤飞一片雪，
百里见秋毫。

No. 1

The eighth moon, the border wind blows;
The Hun hawks fly, their white plume glows.
A flake of snow flies up and down;
It sees a hair, a score miles blown.

* Hun: one of barbaric nomadic Asian peoples who frequently invaded China, a general term referring to all northern or western invaders or aliens; Hun, as an adjective or attributive, refers to something about or of Huns.

其 二

寒冬十二月，
苍鹰八九毛。
寄言燕雀莫相啅，
自有云霄万里高。

No. 2

The twelfth moon, it is winter cold;
The hawk's plume is much clipped, behold.
It says to sparrows: Don't chit-cat, chit-chat;
I'll fly thousands of miles high, high like that.

* sparrow: a small, plain-colored passerine bird related to the finches, grosbeaks and buntings, a very common bird in China, a symbol of insignificance.
* I'll fly thousands of miles high: The poet compares himself to a hawk, which, with much plumage clipped, will fly high, despising chit-chatting sparrows.

观博平王志安少府山水粉图

粉壁为空天,
丹青状江海。
游云不知归,
日见白鸥在。
博平真人王志安,
沈吟至此愿挂冠。
松溪石磴带秋色,
愁客思归坐晓寒。

Appreciating the Mountain-River Water Color Painting of Chih-an Wang, Magistrate of Broadpeace

For the sky the wall's painted blue;
Streams and seas fit your indigo.
The clouds can't return, now astray,
White seagulls come day after day.
A true man in Broadpeace is Chih-an, my friend;
His hat put off, from power he will descend.
The pine brook and stone steps in autumn hue,
Sitting in dawning chill, back home I'd go.

* seagull: a kind of sea bird, any gull or large tern, a symbol of clean integrity. The seagulls in the Wordist book *Sir Line* (Liehtzu) are particularly sensitive to impurity of motive and will make friends only with the completely guileless and disinterested.
* Broadpeace: an ancient town located in present-day Liaoch'eng, Shantung Province.
* Chih-an: referring to Chih-an Wang, Pai Li's friend, the magistrate of Broadpeace.

题雍丘崔明府丹灶

美人为政本忘机，
服药求仙事不违。
叶县已泥丹灶毕，
瀛洲当伴赤松归。
先师有诀神将助，
大圣无心火自飞。
九转但能生羽翼，
双凫忽去定何依。

An Inscription for Red Forge of Ts'ui, Magistrate of Pondknoll

A virtuous man has no craft in court;
Service does not immortality thwart.
In Yeh a cinnabar forge has been made;
You should join Red Pine in the fairy glade.
Master, with his knack, could on God rely;
The saint, not biased, lets the stove fire fly.
With the elixir, plumage one can grow;
The two mallards in flight, where will they go?

* Pondknoll: an ancient town in today's Honan Province.
* Yeh: a county in today's Honan Province.
* cinnabar forge: a forge for refining elixir in Wordist alchemy with cinnabar, a crystallized red mercuric sulfide, HgS, the chief ore of mercury.
* Red Pine: an immortal who named himself Red Pine, formerly a shepherd called Ch'uping Huang, who was admired by a Wordist for his good deeds and brought to Mt.

Gold Bloom to learn the Word.

* glade: a clearing or open space in a wood. Natural places like coves, glades, hills, moors, rivers, mounts and seas, and so on often allude to reclusion in Chinese culture.

观元丹丘坐巫山屏风

昔游三峡见巫山，
见画巫山宛相似。
疑是天边十二峰，
飞入君家彩屏里。
寒松萧瑟如有声，
阳台微茫如有情。
锦衾瑶席何寂寂，
楚王神女徒盈盈。
高咫尺，如千里，
翠屏丹崖粲如绮。
苍苍远树围荆门，
历历行舟泛巴水。
水石潺湲万壑分，
烟光草色俱氛氲。
溪花笑日何年发，
江客听猿几岁闻。
使人对此心缅邈，
疑入嵩丘梦彩云。

Watching Redknoll Yüan Sitting Before a Screen of Mt. Witch

I saw Witch when in Three Gorges I did row,
To Witch this painting is exactly true.
Did the twelve peaks at the end of the sky
Rise and to the colored screen of yours fly?

The cold pines sough as if they produce sound;
Sun Mound o'er there seems to have love profound.
How lone the silk quilt and jade mat remain!
King of Ch'u and Nymph had their tryst in vain.
The little screen covers thousands of miles,
Where verdant hills and red crags beam with smiles.
Chastegate is shaded by the distant trees;
The boats one by one Pa's blue water crease.
Streams from the valleys gurgle on the stone;
The mist touches the grass with a soft tone.
Which day did the creek-by blooms start to burst;
Which year did rowers hear monkeys cry first?
Before the painting I feel refreshed out;
I may have met gods in my dream I doubt.

* Redknoll Yüan: a Wordist and an important friend of Pai Li's. Pai Li met him at the age of twenty and once lived in seclusion with him on Mt. Tower.
* Witch: Mt. Witch, a mythical and religious mountain, which was thought to be a range of mountains in present-day Sha'anhsi Province.
* Sun Mound: the place where Goddess of Mt. Witch dated with King Hsiang of Ch'u (? – 263 B.C.).
* King of Ch'u: probably referring to King Huai of Ch'u (374 B.C.– 296 B.C.).
* Nymph: referring to Goddess of Mt. Witch, a beautiful fairy dwelling on Mt. Witch, who shaped herself as clouds at dawn and turned into rain at dusk. In myths, King Huai of Ch'u once met her in his dream, and had an intercourse overnight. The story was recorded by Jade Sung, a student of Yüan Ch'ü's, when he travelled to Cloud Dream Moor with King Hsiang.
* Chastegate: a town located on the southern bank of the Yangtze River, today's Hupei Province.
* Pa: referring to the Pa River in today's Yellow Mound (Huangkang), originating from the top of Mt. West on the border between today's Hupei and Anhui, flowing 148 kilometers before joining the the Long River.

求崔山人百丈崖瀑布图

百丈素崖裂，
四山丹壁开。
龙潭中喷射，
昼夜生风雷。
但见瀑泉落，
如潄云汉来。
闻君写真图，
岛屿备萦回。
石黛刷幽草，
曾青泽古苔。
幽缄倘相传，
何必向天台。

Asking for a Highcliff-Waterfall Painting from Ts'ui, the Hermit

Highcliff Waterfall does cliffs crack;
The red crags do all-round air hack.
The dragon abyss does there spray,
Thundering and lightening all day.
The cataract from above rushes;
As if the Milky Way down flushes.
I hear in this picture of yours,
Isle after isle, mist like smoke soars.
Your graphite does the grass emboss;
Your bluestone profiles the old moss.

Hide it? Give it to me, a gift;
I needn't tour there, mount or rift.

* Highcliff Waterfall: in today's Weifang, Shantung Province. Meandering up about a mile from the Wen River one finds High-cliff Waterfall in a giant ravine called Waterfall Dale or Silver River Dale.
* the Milky Way: the Silver River literally in Chinese, a river made by Queen Mother with her hair pin according to Chinese mythology; physically, a luminous band circling the heavens composed of stars and nebulae; the Galaxy.
* moss: a tiny, delicate green bryophytic plant growing on damp decaying wood, wet ground, humid rocks or trees, producing capsules which open by an operculum and contain spores. Under a poet's writing brush, it may arouse a poetic feeling or imagination.

见野草中有白头翁者

醉入田家去,
行歌荒野中。
如何青草里,
亦有白头翁?
折取对明镜,
宛将衰鬓同。
微芳似相诮,
留恨向东风。

Windflowers Appear in the Grass

Drunk, to a farmer's house I reel;
Singing in the wild, high I feel.
How in the grass, I find it queer,
Is it that windflowers there appear?
I take a glass and I look there;
They are the same with my white hair.
It seems e'en the grass sneers at me:
With the east wind your prime does flee.

* windflower: the rue anemone that buds into white flowers, like the white hair of an old man.

流夜郎题葵叶

惭君能卫足，
叹我远移根。
白日如分照，
还归守故园。

Inscription for a Mallow Leaf in Nightboy

I admire you: you can there stay;
I sigh I've strayed here all the way.
If the white sun can shed light down,
I must go back to my old town.

* Nightboy: once the biggest country in the southwest that existed about 300 years till the Han dynasty, covering today's Kuichow and a part of Hunan and Kuanghsi provinces. When a Han envoy visited Nigthboy, the king asked: "Which is bigger, Nigthboy or Han?" This self-important question has been a laughing stock ever since. In 27 B.C., Nightboy was wiped out by the Han Empire and was made a county.

莹禅师房观山海图

真僧闭精宇，
灭迹含达观。
列嶂图云山，
攒峰入霄汉。
丹崖森在目，
清昼疑卷幔。
蓬壶来轩窗，
瀛海入几案。
烟涛争喷薄，
岛屿相凌乱。
征帆飘空中，
瀑水洒天半。
峥嵘若可陟，
想像徒盈叹。
杳与真心冥，
遂谐静者玩。
如登赤城里，
揭步沧洲畔。
即事能娱人，
从兹得萧散。

Viewing the Painting of Mountains and Seas in Ying's Zen Room

In the hall you chant, calm your face;
You are free, having left no trace.

The mountains tower tall with clouds high;
A cluster of peaks pierce the sky.
The red cliffs through the mist unfold;
All sights are seen, like screen up rolled.
To my window Three Isles appear;
And to my desk East Sea comes near.
The misty waves surge up, express;
The islands are mixed, in a mess.
The white sails seem to flow on high;
The waterfall drops down from the sky.
The steep mountains if I can scale,
In my mind's eye I may loud wail.
At this painting I feel my soul;
Wherein calmness is calm's goal.
To be climbing Red Town I seem,
Or strolling Blue Shoal like a dream.
The scenery can all people please,
So that they, of course, rest at ease.

* Zen room: a room in which Zen is practiced. Zen is a kind of performance of quietude in a form of meditation or contemplation. When the Sanskrit word jana was introduced to Chinese culture, it was translated as Zan or Zen for this kind of practice.
* Three Isles: referring to the three fairy islands in East Sea.
* East Sea: what is called East China Sea now, more than 700,000 square kilometers.
* Red Town: Mt. Red Town, a mountain located in present-day Shaohsing (Chechiang Province), so named because of the red soil covering the land.
* Blue Shoal: an ancient town near Rising Bay in today's Hopei Province.

白 鹭 鸶

白鹭下秋水，
孤飞如坠霜。
心闲且未去，
独立沙洲傍。

The White Egret

The egret lights on the chill stream,
Like a flake flies in frosty gleam.
It lingers there, what a free soul,
Or stands alone beside the shoal!

* egret: a heron characterized by long and loose plumes drooping over the tail, usually white plumage, an important image in Chinese literature.

咏　槿

园花笑芳年，
池草艳春色。
犹不如槿花，
婵娟玉阶侧。
芬荣何夭促，
零落在瞬息。
岂若琼树枝，
终岁长翕赩。

Ode to the Hibiscus

The garden blooms smile to their prime;
The pool grass does outshine spring thyme.
The hibiscus, the best of all,
By the jade steps does one enthrall.
Blooming so short, like in a rush,
The blossoms fade fast from their blush.
There's nothing like the emerald pine
That's green all year round with its shine.

* thyme: any of a genus of small shrubby plants of the mint family, having aromatic leaves and cultivated for seasoning in cookery.
* hibiscus: any of various malvaceous herbs, shrubs and trees of the genus *Hibiscus*, having large, showy flowers of various colors.
* jade steps: the steps before, and leading to, a palace hall, often used as a metonymy for the court.

咏　桂

世人种桃李，
皆在金张门。
攀折争捷径，
及此春风暄。
一朝天霜下，
荣耀难久存。
安知南山桂，
绿叶垂芳根。
清阴亦可托，
何惜树君园。

Ode to the Laurel

All the world plant peaches and plums;
From the Chins or Changs the best comes.
Everyone will the best spray pluck,
And in the spring riots try his luck.
Howe'er, when all is touched with frost,
Their gleam or glory will be lost.
Who knows laurels on the South Mound
Remain green all o'er all year round.
Though to their shade you may resort,
Why don't you plant some in your court?

* laurel: an evergreen shrub with aromatic, lance-shaped leaves, yellowish flowers, and succulent, cherry-like fruit, a symbol of glory usually in the form of a crown or wreath

of laurel to indicate honor or high merit, especially when one had passed Grand Test, i.e. Civil Service Examinations for selecting government officials, in ancient China. In Chinese mythology, there is a laurel tree on the moon, and it would never fall even though Kang Wu has kept cutting it.

* peaches and plums: a metonymy for plants in general; a metaphor for disciples or students, and sometimes symbolizing a flashy life.
* the Chins or Changs: a metonymy for rich and powerful families or influential officials. The Changs and the Chins, two powerful families in the Han dynasty, enjoyed long-time prosperity for seven generations.

白　胡　桃

红罗袖里分明见，
白玉盘中看却无。
疑是老僧休念诵，
腕前推下水精珠。

A White Chestnut

In her red sleeve it does look clear and white;
It seems like none in the plate of jade bright!
It seems a monk stops the sutra he reads,
And off his wrist takes down his crystal beads.

* a white chestnut: It might be a bead or some other jewel in the shape of a white chestnut based on the text.
* sutra: a formulated doctrine, often so short as to be unintelligible without a key; literally a rule or a precept. In Buddhism, an extended writing usually in verse, and often in dialogue form, embodying important religious and philosophical propositions, sometimes directly, sometimes in highly allegorical or metaphorical language. The best example is a dialogue between two monks, Hsiu Shen and Neng Hui. The former's verse is like this: "The body is a Bodhi tree; / The mind's like a mirror stand bright. / Make it clean, as oft as can be, / In case dust should on it alight." And Neng Hui replied, bettering the former: "There's nothing like a Bodhi tree, / Nor such things as a mirror stand. / There is nothing that you can see. / Where can dust find a place to land?"

巫 山 枕 障

巫山枕障画高丘，
白帝城边树色秋。
朝云夜入无行处，
巴水横天更不流。

Mt. Witch Painted on the Screen

Mt. Witch with its peek painted on the screen,
The autumn chills Whitegod and the trees green.
Dawning clouds befall the night I don't know;
The Pa links the sky with its unseen flow.

* screen: a curtain or shelter, which separates or cuts off, shelters or protects as a light partition, a common image in Chinese literature. Two lines from a Sung lyric by Haowen Yüan reads like this: "The drizzle falls before my tower's sill; / 'Broidered with crabapples, the screen's chill."
* Mt. Witch: a mythical and religious mountain, which was thought to be a range of mountains in Sha'anhsi.
* Whitegod: an ancient city built by Shu Lordson (? – A.D. 36) at the end of the Western Han dynasty, located near present-day Double Gain (Ch'ungch'ing). It is famous in history as the place where Pei Liu, the Emperor of Shu, died in the Three Kingdoms Period (A.D. 220 – A.D. 280).

南奔书怀

遥夜何漫漫，
空歌白石烂。
宁戚未匡齐，
陈平终佐汉。
欃枪扫河洛，
直割鸿沟半。
历数方未迁，
云雷屡多难。
天人秉旄钺，
虎竹光藩翰。
侍笔黄金台，
传觞青玉案。
不因秋风起，
自有思归叹。
主将动谗疑，
王师忽离叛。
自来白沙上，
鼓噪丹阳岸。
宾御如浮云，
从风各消散。
舟中指可掬，
城上骸争爨。
草草出近关，
行行昧前算。
南奔剧星火，
北寇无涯畔。
顾乏七宝鞭，

留连道傍玩。
太白夜食昴，
长虹日中贯。
秦赵兴天兵，
茫茫九州乱。
感遇明主恩，
颇高祖逊言。
过江誓流水，
志在清中原。
拔剑击前柱，
悲歌难重论。

An Impromptu While I Flee Down South

The long night lingers on and on;
In vain I sing *Shining White Stone*.
Ning did the State of Ch'i lead;
Ch'en did in helping Han succeed.
The comet sweeps the Lo far and wide,
And makes a chasm to the world divide.
T'ang is not finished yet while now
There are still disasters enow.
Prince of Peace does a halberd hold;
Seal in hand, he'll the state remold.
On Golden Mound a writ I write,
With wine on the desk shining bright.
It's not because autumn wind blows
That my thought back to the hills goes.
Between generals rise suspicions,
Hence the troops fall to rebellions.

Since I came to the shoal, White Sand,
Noise has quaked Redshine on the land.
Guests and guards like clouds thereon swell;
A wind blows them to flee, pell-mell.
Fingers cut off fill a whole boat;
O'er the wall, bone smoke curls, afloat.
Out of the pass the soldiers flee,
Back? Forth? In dilemma they be.
Down south it's hard and war fire glows;
Without bound there swarm northern foes.
I look around, no whip to sway;
The chasers are barred to delay.
Venus does the Pleiades invade;
The rainbow long does the sun raid.
Ch'in and Chao now give rise to war,
Hence on the land a great uproar.
To His Majesty sage I bow
And keep in mind General Tsu's vow.
And I take oath to the downpour
That I will the mid-land restore.
With my sword the pillar I strike;
So sad, I'll sing no tune alike.

* *Shining White Stone*: a song that Ch'i Ning sang to Lord Pillar of Ch'i.
* Ning: referring to Ch'i Ning, a senior official of Ch'i in the Spring and Autumn period. Ning was born into a poor family but developed into a meritorious minister that helped Lord Pillar of Ch'i prevail over other states.
* the State of Ch'i: Ch'i (1000 B.C.- 221 B.C.), a vassal state of Chough, a powerful state in the Spring and Autumn period and the Warring States period.
* Ch'en: P'ing Ch'en (? - 178 B.C.), a strategist and one of the founders of Han or Western Han.
* Han: the powerful Han Empire (202 B.C.- A.D. 220) founded by Pang Liu, one of the

greatest empires in Chinese history, earlier than, and concurrent with, the Roman Empire (27 B.C.- A.D. 476), with an area of six million and nine square kilometers, including Korea in the east, Vietnam in the south, Mt. Wild Leek in the west and Gobi in the north.
* Golden Mound: built by King Glare of Yan for attracting talents.
* Redshine: a lake at the lower stretch of the Yangtze River.
* Venus: In Chinese astrology, there will be a disaster when Venus shows up across the sky in the daytime.
* the Pleiades: one the twenty-eight lunar mansions in the sky.
* Ch'in and Chao: The lords of Ch'in and Chao were brothers but became enemy afterwards. It insinuates Heng Li, the later Emperor of T'ang, and Lin Li, Prince E'er. The two royal brothers had a fight for the throne.
* General Tsu: referring to Ti Tsu (A.D. 266 - A.D. 321), a military strategist in the Chin dynasty.

古近体诗八十八首
Old-new Rhythmic Poetry, 88 Poems

题随州紫阳先生壁

神农好长生，
风俗久已成。
复闻紫阳客，
早署丹台名。
喘息餐妙气，
步虚吟真声。
道与古仙合，
心将元化并。
楼疑出蓬海，
鹤似飞玉京。
松雪窗外晓，
池水阶下明。
忽耽笙歌乐，
颇失轩冕情。
终愿惠金液，
提携凌太清。

Inscription for the Wall of Purple Sun from Suichow

The wish for a long life to stay
Started in Magic Farmer's day.
Purple Sun, the saint, as is said
Is lined in *Red Mound*, a book red.
Breathing in and out subtle air,
And chanting a tune, truly fair.

The Way fits what immortals do;
The heart and Nature as one go.
Their towers on Fairy Isle there rise;
A crane will take you to the skies.
The window-by pines face dawn light;
The steps lead to the pool so bright.
I am obsessed with the pipe tune,
Leaving those peers and lords alone.
Give me some gold elixir, pray,
So fly to Great Pure Hall we may.

* Purple Sun: a renowned Wordist in the T'ang dynasty.
* Magic Farmer: one of the Three Sovereigns in remote ages, along with Hidden Spirit and Nüwa. Magic Farmer, also known as King of Corn, is regarded as the father of herb medicine and agriculture.
* *Red Mound* : a book in which immortals are recorded.
* the Way: the other way of saying the Word, the ultimate principle in the universe.
* Fairy Isle: an ideal imaginary place that fairies and immortals live in East Sea.
* Great Pure Hall: indicating realm of real freedom.

题元丹丘山居

故人栖东山，
自爱丘壑美。
青春卧空林，
白日犹不起。
松风清襟袖，
石潭洗心耳。
羡君无纷喧，
高枕碧霞里。

Inscription for Redknoll Yüan's Abode in the Mountains

My friend abides on Mt. Tower east;
With hills and rills he is well pleased.
For all spring in the glade he lies;
E'en at sunrise he does not rise.
His sleeves are cleaned by a pine breeze;
His heart and ears Stone Pool does please.
I admire your life without care,
Your head pillowed on the clouds fair.

* Redknoll Yüan: a Wordist and an important friend of Pai Li's. Pai Li met him at the age of twenty and once lived in seclusion with him on Mt. Tower. Redknoll exerted great influence on Pai Li's ideology in their 22 years of friendship and communication.
* Mt. Tower: one of the Five Sacred Mountains in China, located in today's Honan Province, along with Mt. Ever in Shanhsi, Mt. Arch in Shantung, Mt. Flora in Sha'anhsi, and Mt. Scale in Hunan. It is one of the five sanctuaries of Wordism, and

the abode of God of Mt. Tower worshipped by Han Chinese.
* glade: a clearing or open space in a wood. Natural places like coves, glades, hills, moors, rivers, mounts and seas, and so on often allude to reclusion in Chinese culture.
* Stone Pool: unidentified.

题元丹丘颖阳山居

仙游渡颖水，
访隐同元君。
忽遗苍生望，
独与洪崖群。
卜地初晦迹，
兴言且成文。
却顾北山断，
前瞻南岭分。
遥通汝海月，
不隔嵩丘云。
之子合逸趣，
而我钦清芬。
举迹倚松石，
谈笑迷朝曛。
益愿狎青鸟，
拂衣栖江濆。

Inscription for Redknoll Yüan's Abode in the Mountains in Yingshine

I cross the Ying to find a man,
A hermit, who is my friend Yüan.
Why are you from the world away
And with immortal Great Crag stay?
Quietude is why this place you chose;
Each of your talk can be good prose.

To the north is the mountain chopped;
In the south are the ridges lopped.
The creek and the Ru share the moon;
Mt. Tower and the knolls do commune.
You are so free, resting at ease,
And I imbibe your balmy breeze.
Leaning on the pine stone you can gain,
While laughing at the clouds and rain.
I would get near to the blue birds
Or by the river join the herds.

* Redknoll Yüan: a Wordist and an important friend of Pai Li's. Pai Li met him at the age of twenty and once lived in seclusion with him on Mt. Tower, regarding him as "a free man".
* the Ying: referring to the River Ying, a river derived from Mt. Tower. The River Ying has been regarded as one of the origins of Chinese culture.
* Great Crag: a singer and dancer in the Three Emperors period (6727 B.C.- 3077 B.C.), an immortal.
* the Ru: referring to the Ru River originating from today's Tower County, Loshine Prefecture, Honan Province, a main branch of the Huai River.
* Mt. Tower: one of the Five Sacred Mountains in China, located in present-day Honan Province, along with Mt. Ever in Shanhsi, Mt. Arch in Shantung, Mt. Flora in Sha'anhsi, and Mt. Scale in Hunan.

题瓜洲新河饯族叔舍人贲

齐公凿新河，
万古流不绝。
丰功利生人，
天地同朽灭。
两桥对双阁，
芳树有行列。
爱此如甘棠，
谁云敢攀折。
吴关倚此固，
天险自兹设。
海水落斗门，
潮平见沙汭。
我行送季父，
弭棹徒流悦。
杨花满江来，
疑是龙山雪。
惜此林下兴，
怆为山阳别。
瞻望清路尘，
归来空寂蔑。

Inscription for the New Canal in Melon Shoal While Feasting Fen, My Uncle, the Royal Servant

Lord Ch'i has dug a canal new
That will for timeless ages flow.

To all people it will do good;

Live with Heaven and earth it would.

Two bridges are faced with two towers,

And there lined up are trees and flowers.

These trees are like birchleaf pears;

To pick their twigs or leaves who dares?

Wu's passes will be fortified,

A defense strong from every side.

The sluice bars water from the sea;

The tide ebbs and shoals come to be.

My uncle's going on his way,

I stop the oar for long to stay.

Catkins all o'er the river flow;

I doubt Mt. Dragon sends here snow.

Like the Seven Men in bamboo,

We hate to part, all seeming blue.

Into the dust kicked off I gaze;

Our home, now I think, lonely stays.

* Melon Shoal: a town located in today's Yangchow, Chiangsu Province.
* Lord Ch'i: referring to Huan Ch'i (A.D. 678 – A.D. 750), the prefect of Moist (Junchow), that is, today's Chenchiang, a city of Chiangsu Province.
* birchleaf pear: *Pyrus calleryana Decne*, a perennial tree, having white flowers and brown or reddish fruit.
* catkin: a deciduous scaly spike of flowers, as in the willow, an image of helpless drifting or wandering in Chinese literature.
* Mt. Dragon: a mountain in today's Tangt'u, Anhui Province.
* the Seven Men in bamboo: referring to the Seven Sages of Bamboo Groves, a group of renowned scholars in the Chin dynasty.
* bamboo: a tall, tree-like or shrubby grass in tropical and semi-tropical regions, a symbol of integrity, fortitude and altitude. A Ching poet speaks of its character in a poem *Bamboo Rooted in the Rock*: "You bite the green hill and ne'er rest. / Roots in the broken crag, you grow, / And stand erect although hard pressed. / East, west, south, north, let the wind blow."

洗　脚　亭

白道向姑熟，
洪亭临道傍。
前有昔时井，
下有五丈床。
樵女洗素足，
行人歇金装。
西望白鹭洲，
芦花似朝霜。
送君此时去，
回首泪成行。

Washing Feet by the Pavilion

To Kushu runs the broad way straight;
Nearby stands the pavilion great.
In front, there's a well left before;
Below, a stone fifty feet or more.
A wood girl may wash her feet here;
A passenger may breathe fresh air.
Egret Shoal west it does accost,
Where reed catkins fly like hoarfrost.
You set off on your way, alack,
My tears drip down while I turn back.

* Kushu: a town in today's Tangt'u, Anhui Province.

* Egret Shoal: White Egret Shoal, an ancient shoal in the middle of the Yangtze River.
* catkin: a deciduous scaly spike of flowers, as in the willow, an image of helpless drifting or wandering in Chinese literature.

劳 劳 亭

天下伤心处，
劳劳送客亭。
春风知别苦，
不遣柳条青。

The Farewell Pavilion

The place that does rend one's heart
Is the Farewell Pavilion keen.
Spring wind knows it's bitter to part;
It does not blow the willows green.

* the Farewell Pavilion: 7.5 kilometers from Gold Hill, today's Nanking, Ch'angsu Province.
* willow: any of a large genus of shrubs and trees related to the poplars, having generally smooth branches, and often long, slender, pliant, and sometimes pendent branchlets, a symbol of farewell or nostalgia in Chinese culture. The best image is in *Vetch We Pick*, a verse in *The Book of Songs*, which reads like this: When we left long ago, / The willows waved adieu. / Now back to our home town, / We meet snow falling down.

题金陵王处士水亭

王子耽玄言,
贤豪多在门。
好鹅寻道士,
爱竹啸名园。
树色老荒苑,
池光荡华轩。
此堂见明月,
更忆陆平原。
扫拭青玉簟,
为余置金尊。
醉罢欲归去,
花枝宿鸟喧。
何时复来此,
再得洗嚣烦。

Inscription for the Water Pavilion of Wang, a Hermit, in Gold Hill

You love the profoundest of all;
Gents and gallants swarm in your hall.
You seek hermits and you love geese;
In your yard you hear bamboo breeze.
The old trees have aged the park;
The pool ripples to towers now dark.
In this hall the moon I can see
While Plain Land does occur to me.

My jade mat for me you clean up
And pour wine into my gold cup.
Now so drunk, I would go away;
A bird to perch chirps on a spray.
When can I come back here again,
So that we can clean off our stain?

* Gold Hill: referring to Nanking, one of the most well-known ancient cities in China, a strategic fort as a gateway to the sea, which has been the capital of Wu, Chin, and many other states or kingdoms, such as the six empires called Six Dynasties and has flourished immensely with increasing trade and travel.
* Plain Land: referring to Chi Lu (A.D. 261 – A.D. 303), a renowned litterateur and calligrapher in the Western Chin dynasty. Wang's garden was the former residence of Chi Lu.

题嵩山逸人元丹丘山居

白久在庐、霍,元公近游嵩山,故交深情,出处无间,呙信频及,许为主人,欣然适会本意。当冀长往不返,欲便举家就之,兼书共游,因有此赠。

家本紫云山,
道风未沦落。
沉怀丹丘志,
冲赏归寂寞。
朅来游闽荒,
扪涉穷禹凿。
夤缘泛潮海,
偃蹇陟庐霍。
凭雷蹑天窗,
弄景憩霞阁。
且欣登眺美,
颇惬隐沦诺。
三山旷幽期,
四岳聊所托。
故人契嵩颍,
高义炳丹臒。
灭迹遗纷嚣,
终言本峰壑。
自矜林湍好,
不羡朝市乐。
偶与真意并,
顿觉世情薄。
尔能折芳桂,
吾亦采兰若。

拙妻好乘鸾,
娇女爱飞鹤。
提携访神仙,
从此炼金药。

Inscription for the Mountain Abode of Redknoll Yüan, a Hermit on Mt. Tower

I've toured Mt. Lodge and Mt. Scale for some time while my best and intimate friend Yüan is touring Mt. Tower. We write to each other quite often and he invites me to his place and I accept it happily. I wish to stay with him for long and move my family there so that I can write and travel with him, hence this poem.

Mt. Purple Clouds there you dwelt on,
Your love for the Word not yet gone.
To mountains you'd often retire;
Quiet leisure is what you desire.
You travelled to the southern clime
To find Worm's trace left from that time.
You managed to chase wave and tide
And on Mt. Lodge and Mt. Scale bide.
A thunder sent news from the sky;
Your pavilion kissed clouds on high.
You climbed to enjoy sights so good
And took delight in the deep wood.
Three mountains were what you loved best;
Four valleys were where you would rest.
Hills and rills were where you'd resort;
Your holiness e'en raised the court.

From the bustle you keep away;
And in woods and dales you will stay.
You take glade pleasure as a must,
Admiring not the worldly lust.
Once you find the Word you live in,
You realize the world is so thin.
You'd like to pick a laurel spray
And the orchid balm is my fay.
My wife loves the phoenix pure;
A crane does my daughter allure.
Keen to join fairies as we are,
Let's start to refine cinnabar!

* Redknoll Yüan: a Wordist and an important friend of Pai Li's. Pai Li met him at the age of twenty and once lived in seclusion with him on Mt. Tower.
* Mt. Tower: one of the Five Sacred Mountains in China, located in Henan Province, along with Mt. Ever in Shanhsi, Mt. Arch in Shantung, Mt. Flora in Sha'anhsi, and Mt. Scale in Hunan. It is one of the five sanctuaries of Wordism, and the abode of God of Mt. Tower worshipped by Han Chinese.
* Worm: the founder and the first king of Hsia, who took over the leadership from Hibiscus.
* Mt. Lodge: a famous mountain with historic, cultural and religious attractions, located in present-day Chianghsi Province.
* Mt. Scale: one of the Five Mountains in China, located in Hunan Province, along with Mt. Ever in Shanhsi, Mt. Arch in Shantung, Mt. Flora in Sha'anhsi, and Mt. Tower in Honan.
* Mt. Purple Cloud: a mountain in the poet's hometown, Mienchow, located on the gateway to Ch'engtu.
* the Word: referring to Tao if transliterated, the most significant and profoundest concept in Chinese philosophy, comparable to the Word or the Logos in western cosmology.
* glade: a clearing or open space in a luxuriant wood. Natural places like coves, glades, hills, moors, rivers, mounts and seas, and so on often allude to reclusion in Chinese culture.

- laurel: an evergreen shrub with aromatic, lance-shaped leaves, yellowish flowers, and succulent, cherry-like fruit, a symbol of glory usually in the form of a crown or wreath of laurel to indicate honor or high merit, especially when one had passed Grand Test in ancient China. In Chinese mythology, there is a laurel tree on the moon, and it would never fall even though Kang Wu has kept cutting it.
- phoenix: In Chinese mythology, the phoenix only perches on phoenix trees, i.e. firmiana, only eats firmiana fruit, and only drinks sweet spring water, and this mythic bird appears only in times of peace and sagacious rule.
- crane: one of a family of large, long-necked, long-legged, heronlike birds allied to the rails, a symbol of integrity and longevity in Chinese culture, only second to the phoenix in cultural importance.

题江夏修静寺

我家北海宅，
作寺南江滨。
空庭无玉树，
高殿坐幽人。
书带留青草，
琴堂幂素尘。
平生种桃李，
寂灭不成春。

Inscription for Quietude Fane in Riversummer

My cousin North Sea's mansion old,
Is a fane by the South. Behold,
In the void court there's no tree tall,
But a monk seated in the hall.
Left in the green grass are book ties;
The lute room collects dust—dust lies.
You've grown lots of peaches by far,
It's no spring, many as they are.

* Quietude Fane: a fane or temple, which had been Prefect North Sea Li's old residence.
* Riversummer: an ancient county, i. e., present-day Riversummer (Chianghsia) District, Wuhan, Hupei Province.
* North Sea: referring to Yung Li (A.D. 678 – A.D. 747), once Prefect of North Sea, a famous poet and calligrapher in the T'ang dynasty. A talented and outspoken official, he was killed by Premier Linfu Li out of schemes and intrigues.

* the South: a river unidentified.
* peach: any of the plant (*Prunus Percica*), bearing a fleshy, juicy, edible drupe, cultivated in many varieties in temperate zones considered sacred in China, often used as a metaphor for a young woman, as a section of a poem in *The Book of Songs* reads: "The peach twigs sway, / Ablaze the flower; / Now she's married away, / Befitting her new bower."

改九子山为九华山联句

　　青阳县有九子山，山高数千丈，上有九峰如莲花。按图征名，无所依据。太史公南游，略而不书。事绝古老之口，复缺名贤之纪，虽灵仙往复，而赋咏罕闻。予削其旧号，加以九华之目。时访道江汉，憩于夏侯回之堂，开檐岸帻，坐眺松雪，因与二三子联句，传之将来。

妙有分二气，
灵山开九华。
层标遏迟日，
半壁明朝霞。
积雪曜阴壑，
飞流喷阳崖。
青莹玉树色，
缥缈羽人家。

A Cooperation on a Verse for Mt. Nine Sons Changed Into Mt. Nine Flowers

　　In Greenshine County rolls Mt. Nine Sons, which is more than ten thousand meters high, with nine peaks looking like lotus flowers. Its name and look do not match. When Grand Historiographer toured here, he did not write about it. There are no ancient records or writings by celebrities. Though spirits come and go, there are few poems in praise of it. I delete the old name and rename it Mt. Nine Flowers. Now on my tour to the Long River and the Han River, I rest in the Hall of Hui Hisahou. Kerchief pulled back from forehead, I sit, looking at the pine snow and cooperate with a few friends in writing a poem to be passed on to posterity.

Shade and Shine turn into good hours;
The holy mountains burst: Nine Flowers.
The tall tower bars light of the sun;
On half the wall dawning clouds run.
The dale's lit up by the piled snow;
The cliff's refined by a thrown flow.
The emerald tree does brightly shine;
Where immortals on nectar dine.

* Mt. Nine Flowers: one of the Four Buddhist Mountains in China in present-day Anhui Province.
* Greenshine County: a county in present-day Anhui Province near Mt. Nine Flowers.
* Grand Historiographer: Chien Ssuma (145 B.C.- 90 B.C.), a great historiographer, litterateur, and thinker in the Western Han dynasty.
* the Long River: the longest river in China, originating from the T'angkula Mountains on Tibet Plateau, flowing through 11 provincial areas, more than 6,300 kilometers long, the third longest river in the world.
* the Han River: the longest branch of the Long River, which originates in Sha'anhsi and flows southwestward through Hupei, joining the main stream in today's Wuhan.
* Shade and Shine: the most important and basic concept of Chinese or Eastern philosophy, characterized by three features: identification, opposition and interconversion, although apparently standing for two poles of binary opposition.

题 宛 溪 馆

吾怜宛溪好，
百尺照心明。
何谢新安水，
千寻见底清。
白沙留月色，
绿竹助秋声。
却笑严湍上，
于今独擅名。

Inscription for Wan Stream Mansion

I love the Wan Stream brightly fine;
The hundred-feet depth cleans heart mine.
With New Peace it can well compare,
Limpid to the bed, clearly fair.
The white sand keeps hues of the moon;
The bamboo helps the autumn tune.
What fun! Yantse Shoal enjoys fame;
Should it monopolize the name?

* The Wan Stream: located north of Gold Hill.
* New Peace: a river located in the upper stretch of the Ch'ient'ang River, deriving from Anhui.
* bamboo: a tall, tree-like or shrubby grass in tropical and semi-tropical regions, a symbol of integrity and altitude, one of the four most important images in Chinese literature, which are wintersweet, orchid, bamboo, and chrysanthemum.
* Yantse Shoal: where Tsuling Yan (39 B.C.- A.D. 41) used to fish. Tsuling Yan was a

renowned hermit in the Han dynasty. He showed his talent at an early age. After Hsiu Liu was enthroned to be the emperor of Han, Yan was invited several times to serve the court. Though the emperor was an acquaintance of his, Yan declined the offer and chose to live in seclusion in the Richspring Hills.

题东溪公幽居

杜陵贤人清且廉,
东豀卜筑岁将淹。
宅近青山同谢朓,
门垂碧柳似陶潜。
好鸟迎春歌后院,
飞花送酒舞前檐。
客到但知留一醉,
盘中只有水晶盐。

Inscription for Lord East Stream's Villa

The sage on Tu's Ridge is upright and clean;
Since his east stream building, years it has been.
His estate near the green hill is like T'iao's;
The gate-by drooping willows outshine T'ao's.
The cute birds greet spring in the yard: hi, hi;
The petals, sending wine to the eaves, fly.
I urge new guests: drink it, don't hesitate,
Though there is but crystal salt in the plate.

* Tu's Ridge: located on the southeast of Long Peace, the capital of T'ang.
* T'iao: referring to T'iao Hsieh (A.D. 464 – A.D. 499), an outstanding highborn landscape poet from Southern Ch'i (A.D. 479 – A.D.502) in the Southern Dynasties period.
* T'ao: referring to Poolbright T'ao (A.D. 352 – A.D. 427), a verse writer, poet, and litterateur in the Chin dynasty, and the founder of Chinese idyllism, who was once the magistrate of P'engtse.

嘲鲁儒

鲁叟谈五经，
白发死章句。
问以经济策，
茫如坠烟雾。
足著远游履，
首戴方山巾。
缓步从直道，
未行先起尘。
秦家丞相府，
不重褒衣人。
君非叔孙通，
与我本殊伦。
时事且未达，
归耕汶水滨。

Sneering at a Lu Confucian

Of *Five Books* Lu's old folk talks much；
He sticks to words and lines as such，
Ask him how a state we can raise，
And he's puzzled as if in haze.
Far-travelling shoes he does wear，
Besides donning a kerchief square.
On the straight road he does tiptoe；
Dust rises when he starts to go.
There in Ch'in's prime minister's hall，

>No such costumed ones stood at all.
>You don't have Shusun's clever mind
>And we are of a different kind.
>As you don't know the world and men,
>Why not plough by the River Wen?

* *Five Books*: referring to the five Confucian classics, that is, *The Book of Songs*, *The Book of Documents*, *Changes*, *Rites*, *Spring and Autumn Annals*, the oldest books of Chinese civilization, which have been well kept till today.
* Lu's old folk: referring to Confucius, a laughing stock in this poem.
* Ch'in's prime minister: referring to Ssu Li (284 B.C.- 208 B.C.), a renowned statesman, litterateur and calligrapher, whose political ideas have had a profound impact on China and laid the foundation of China's political system for more than two thousand years.
* Shusun: Tung Shunsun (? - cir. 194 B.C.), a Confucian in the later years of the Ch'in Empire and a capable official in the time of Emperor Highsire (256 B.C.- 195 B.C.). He wasted much time before going out to reconstruct a devastated land left by the Ch'in Empire by instituting rites for ancestral temples and civil rites and etiquettes.

惧　谗

二桃杀三士，
讵假剑如霜？
众女妒蛾眉，
双花竞春芳。
魏姝信郑袖，
掩袂对怀王。
一惑巧言子，
朱颜成死伤。
行将泣团扇，
戚戚愁人肠。

Fear for Slander

With two peaches three men were killed;
Do we always need a sword gilt?
All beauties incur women's spite;
Two blooms are fomented to fight.
Lady Way then the queen believed;
So by the king her nose was cleaved.
Once hoodwinked so by a glib tongue,
A belle will be maimed or o'errun.
In the end, to her fan she'll cry,
Tear after tear, sigh after sigh!

* With two peaches three men were killed: There were three military commanders in Ch'i who passed by Ying Yan, an important statesman, thinker, and diplomat,

without respect, so Yan triggered a fight among the three by giving two peaches as an award. The three commanders killed each other for the award.

* Two blooms are fomented to fight: A belle from Way was adored by King Huai of Ch'u. The jealous queen told her that the king did not like her nose and suggested she cover her nose when she met the king. Lady Way trusted her and did as she was told. When the king was baffled with Lady Way's nose, the queen slandered her by telling the king that Lady Way disliked his fetid breath. In a rage, the king cut off Lady Way's nose.

观 猎

太守耀清威，
乘闲弄晚晖。
江沙横猎骑，
山火绕行围。
箭逐云鸿落，
鹰随月兔飞。
不知白日暮，
欢赏夜方归。

Watching Hunting

The magistrate looks spruce and proud;
Now at leisure, he plays a dusk cloud.
The hunters rampage on the shore,
The campfire lit up back and fore.
Shot, a wild goose falls from the sky;
The hawk whoops down for the hare sly.
How time goes the hunters forget;
By midnight they haven't gone back yet.

* the campfire: the fire prepared to frighten animals or fowls in hunting.
* wild goose: an undomesticated goose that is caring and responsible, taken as a symbol of benevolence, righteousness, good manner, wisdom, and faith in Chinese culture.
* hawk: a diurnal bird of prey, notable for keen sight and strong flight, usually used as a metaphor for one who takes military means in contrast with a dove, one who tries to find peaceful solutions.

* hare: a rodent (genus *Lepus*) with cleft upper lip, long ears, and long hind legs, characterized by its timidity and swiftness, habitating woodland, farmland or grassland.

观胡人吹笛

胡人吹玉笛，
一半是秦声。
十月吴山晓，
梅花落敬亭。
愁闻出塞曲，
泪满逐臣缨。
却望长安道，
空怀恋主情。

Watching the Hun Man Playing the Pipe

Now the Hun man plays the jade pipe;
Half the melody's of Ch'in type.
Wu's Hills see dawning, now tenth moon;
Chingt'ing hears a *Wintersweet* tune.
I hark to *Out Fortress* with sighs;
My hat lash holds tears from my eyes.
To the road to Long Peace I gaze;
My heart for the lord in vain rays.

* Ch'in: about and of the Ch'in State or the State of Ch'in.
* Chingt'ing: an offset of Mt. Yellow, consisting of 60 peaks, rolling more than three miles and 317 meters above sea level, a mountain with many literary legacies.
* Wu's Hills: the southern hills in the area that once belonged to the State of Wu.
* *Wintersweet*: a Ch'iang flute tune.
* *Out Fortress*: a Hun tune introduced to China by Ch'ien Chang (164 B.C.- 114 B.C.)
* Long Peace: referring to Ch'ang'an if transliterated, the metropolis of gold, the

capital of the T'ang Empire, with 1,000,000 inhabitants, the largest walled city ever built by man, and a cosmopolis of world religions, Buddhism, Confucianism, Wordism, Nestorianism, Zoroastrianism, and even Islamism represented by Saracens. It saw the wonder of the age that reached the pinnacle of brilliance in Emperor Deepsire's reign: The main castle with its nine-fold gates, the thirty-six imperial palaces, pillars of gold, innumerable mansions and villas of noblemen, the broad avenues thronged with motley crowds of townsfolk, gallants on horseback, and mandarin cars drawn by yokes of black oxen, countless houses of pleasure, which opened their doors by night all made this city a kaleidoscope of miracles.

军　行

骝马新跨白玉鞍，
战罢沙场月色寒。
城头铁鼓声犹震，
匣里金刀血未干。

The General

He rides his steed saddled with jade white;
The battlefield's quiet in the moon's cold light.
The war drum on the wall stops with a thud;
His sword in the casket is stained with blood.

* steed: a horse; especially a spirited war horse. The use of horses in war can be traced back to the Shang dynasty (1600 B.C.- 1046 B.C.), when a department of horse management was established. A verse from *The Book of Songs* tells of Lord Civil of Watch's industriousness: "In state affairs he leads; / He has three thousand steeds."
* saddled with jade white: a fine horse is usually harnessed with gold and saddled with jade.

从 军 行

百战沙场碎铁衣，
城南已合数重围。
突营射杀呼延将，
独领残兵千骑归。

A War Poem

Myriad battles have worn his armor out;
The south of the town's besieged by lines stout.
Shooting the general against his attack,
He leads a thousand remnant horses back.

* horse: a large herbivorous solid-hoofed quadruped (*Equus caballus*) with coarse mane and tail, of various strains: Ferghana, Mongolian, Kazaks, Hequ, Karasahr and so on and of various colors: black, white, yellow, brown, dappled and so on, domesticated about four thousand years go, reared as a pet, employed as a beast of draught and burden and especially for riding upon. Horses have played an important part in human civilization, widely employed in agriculture, transportation and warfare.

平虏将军妻

平虏将军妇，
入门二十年。
君心自有悦，
妾宠岂能专。
出解床前帐，
行吟道上篇。
古人不唾井，
莫忘昔缠绵。

Beat Foe General's Wife

Beat Foe General's wife in tears
Has been with him for twenty years.
He has changed and forgot his vow,
Obsessed with a concubine now.
With her bed net she's leaving soon;
On the way a verse she does croon.
Ancients did not forget the past;
Remember how we've clung fast.

* Beat Foe General: title of a military commander in ancient China.
* concubine: a cohabitant or secondary wife. China was a polygamous society from prehistoric years till the first half of the twentieth century. An ordinary man could have three wives and four concubines and a concubine could be bartered or sold or given as a gift in ancient China. An emperor might have thousands of concubines, for example, Emperor Deepsire had 40,000.

春夜洛城闻笛

谁家玉笛暗飞声,
散入春风满洛城。
此夜曲中闻折柳,
何人不起故园情。

Listening to the Flute in Loshine on a Spring Night

From whose flute flows here a song of sorrow
That steals downtown with a zephyr to roam?
Tonight at this tune of *Breaking Willow*,
Who could restrain his nostalgia for home?

* Loshine: Loyang if transliterated, the second largest city and Eastern Capital of the T'ang Empire.
* *Breaking Willow*: an ancient tune that usually express grief of parting, listed among twenty-four airs for the flute by Conservatoire of Han. Breaking off withies from a willow on the riverbank by a certain bridge outside Long Peace has been used as a symbol of reluctant parting.

嵩山采菖蒲者

神仙多古貌，
双耳下垂肩。
嵩岳逢汉武，
疑是九疑仙。
我来采菖蒲，
服食可延年。
言终忽不见，
灭影入云烟。
喻帝竟莫悟，
终归茂陵田。

A Bulrush Gatherer on Mt. Tower

Fairies look like chaste, as appears;
Shoulder length or so are their ears.
On Mt. Tower one tells Lord Martial:
"It's true, I'm Nine Doubts immortal.
I've come here to pick bulrush fine;
You'd live long if on it you dine."
Then he disappears while he says,
A vague shadow left in the haze.
The lord does not him understand
And turns out dust in that ridge land.

* Mt. Tower: one of the Sacred Five Mountains in China, located in Honan Province, along with Mt. Ever in Shanhsi, Mt. Arch in Shantung, Mt. Flora in Sha'anhsi, and

Mt. Scale in Hunan. It is one of the five sanctuaries of Wordism, and the abode of God of Mt. Tower worshipped by Han Chinese, with an area of 450 square kilometers, consisting of Mt. Greatroom and Mt. Smallroom, having 72 peaks, 350 meters above sea level at the lowest and 1,512 meters at the highest.

* Lord Martial: Emperor Martial (156 B.C.- 87 B.C.), the seventh emperor of Han, a prominent statesman, strategist and poet, and a pursuer of immortality as well.
* Nine Doubts: the mountain where Hibiscus was buried, located in today's Hunan Province. It was so named because it confused people by similar peaks and landscape.
* bulrush: a tall, rushlike plant growing in damp ground or water, such as the tall sedge.

金陵听韩侍御吹笛

韩公吹玉笛,
倜傥流英音。
风吹绕钟山,
万壑皆龙吟。
王子停凤管,
师襄掩瑶琴。
馀韵度江去,
天涯安可寻?

Listening to Han, the Royal Servant, Who Plays the Pipe in Gold Hill

Mister Han plays the pipe: coo, woo;
Spruce, elegant, his voice flows true.
The zephyr does Mt. Bell surround;
All vales with dragons' trills resound.
If a prince heard this tune of flute,
Master Shih-hsiang would stop his lute.
The tune has crossed the river now;
It's far off, where to find it? How?

* Gold Hill: referring to Nanking, one of the most well-known ancient cities in China, a strategic fort as a gateway to the sea, which has been the capital of Wu, Chin, and many other states or kingdoms, such as the six empires called Six Dynasties and has flourished immensely with increasing trade and travel.
* Mt. Bell: located in the east of Gold Hill in present-day Nanking.
* dragon: a fabulous serpent-like giant winged animal that can change its girth and

length, a totem of the Chinese nation, a symbol of benevolence and sovereignty in Chinese culture.
* Master Shih-hsiang: a musician of Lu in the Spring and Autumn period.

流夜郎闻酺不预

北阙圣人歌太康，
南冠君子窜遐荒。
汉酺闻奏钧天乐，
愿得风吹到夜郎。

Exiled in Nightboy and Unable to Attend a Symposium

The saints in the court sing of the great time
While I'm now exiled south to a wild clime.
A blessed symposium tune is played I hear;
May a zephyr blow it to Nightboy here.

* Nightboy: once the biggest kingdom founded by southern barbarians in the southwest existing for about 300 years, from the Warring States period to the Han dynasty. When a Han envoy visited Nigthboy, the king asked:"Which is bigger, Nigthboy or Han?" This self-important question has been a laughing stock ever since. In 27 B.C., Nightboy was wiped out by Han and was instituted as a county.

放后遇恩不沾

天作云与雷，
霈然德泽开。
东风日本至，
白雉越裳来。
独弃长沙国，
三年未许回。
何时入宣室，
更问洛阳才。

Exiled and Not Pardoned

Lightning and thunder in the sky,
The great grace of spring rain comes by.
The east wind up to Japan blows
And to Vietnam this zephyr goes.
I'm exiled in Long Sand, alack,
It's three years and I can't go back.
When can I be summoned, what day
So my talent I could display?

* Long Sand: Ch'angsha if transliterated, a vassal state in the Han dynasty, now the capital city of present-day Hunan Province.

宣城见杜鹃花

蜀国曾闻子规鸟，
宣城还见杜鹃花。
一叫一回肠一断，
三春三月忆三巴。

Seeing Azaleas in Hsuan

In Shu I used to hear cuckoos coo, coo;
Now in Hsuan here, I see azaleas blow.
A cry, a sigh, and a heart breaking down;
The spring, the month, and the dream of my town.

* Hsuan: an ancient town in present-day Hsuan, Anhui Province, a county instituted in the early years of the Ch'in Emperor under the Prefecture of Redshine. It became a prefecture in 281 during the Chin dynasty. It is well known for rich historical legacies, and best remembered for its high-quality rice paper.
* Shu: one of the earliest kingdoms in China, founded by Silkworm according to legend. In the Three Kingdoms period, a new Shu was established by Pei Liu, hence one of the three kingdoms in that period.
* cuckoo: any of a family of birds with a long, slender body, grayish-brown on top and white below, a symbol of sadness in Chinese culture. As is said, during the Shang dynasty, Cuckoo (Yü Tu), a caring king of Shu, abdicated the throne due to a flood and lived in reclusion. After his death, he turned into a cuckoo, wailing day and night, shedding tears and blood.

白田马上闻莺

黄鹂啄紫椹，
五月鸣桑枝。
我行不记日，
误作阳春时。
蚕老客未归，
白田已缫丝。
驱马又前去，
扣心空自悲。

Hearing Orioles Chirp on My Horse at White Field

Orioles peck mulberries in May
And chirp merrily on each spray.
What day I don't know, I just go;
Is it still early spring? O no!
Silkworms old, but I am still out;
Silk reeling they're busy about.
I'd spur my horse to go ahead,
But I could only sigh instead.

* oriole: golden oriole, one of the family of passerine birds, which looks bright yellow with contrasting black wings and sings beautiful songs.
* horse: a large herbivorous solid-hoofed quadruped (Equus caballus) with coarse mane and tail, of various strains: Ferghana, Mongolian, Kazaks, Hequ, Karasahr and so on and of various colors: black, white, yellow, brown, dappled and so on, domesticated about four thousand years go, reared as a pet, employed as a beast of draught and

burden and especially for riding upon. Horses have played an important part in human civilization, widely employed in agriculture, transportation and warefare.
* White Field: White Field Ferry, a ferry in present-day Paoying County, Chiangsu Province.
* mulberry: the edible, berry-like fruit of a tree (genus *Morus*) whose leaves are valued for silkworm culture, and the tree itself, first cultivated in the drainage area of the Yellow River in China about five thousand years ago, concurrent with the time when silkworms were raised.
* silkworm: the larva of a moth that produces a dense silken cocoon, especially the common silkworm from whose cocoon commercial silk is made. The silkworm was cultivated in 3000 B.C. when Lace Mum, who was Lord Yellow's concubine began to raise silkworms and make silk.

三五七言

秋风清，
秋月明，
落叶聚还散，
寒鸦栖复惊，
相思相见知何日，
此时此夜难为情。

Three, Five and Seven Words

Autumn wind brisk;
Autumn moon bright.
Fallen leaves gather and disperse;
Perching ravens all branches fright.
Yearning, burning, I wait for our day;
Annoyed, destroyed, I spend a sad night.

* Three, Five and Seven Words: the poem is arranged with 3 words each line, 5 words each line, and 7 words each line for every two lines.
* raven: a large omnivorous, crow-like bird (*Corvus corax*), having lustrous black plumage, with the feathers of the throat elongated and lanceolate.

杂　　诗

白日与明月，
昼夜尚不闲。
况尔悠悠人，
安得久世间。
传闻海水上，
乃有蓬莱山。
玉树生绿叶，
灵仙每登攀。
一食驻玄发，
再食留红颜。
吾欲从此去，
去之无时还。

Miscellany

Lo, the bright moon, lo the white sun,
Day and night, without stop they run.
How can people busy all day
And in this dust world for e'er stay?
In the ocean, East Sea, I hear
Looms a Fairyland over there.
Emerald trees luxuriant leaves grow;
Fairies to feasts on high oft go.
Eating berries, you've no hair gray,
And more eaten, you'll in prime stay.
Now I am leaving here, alack,

I don't know when I can come back.

* East Sea: what is known as East China Sea today, with an area of 770 thousand square kilometers.
* Fairyland: a legendary ideal abode for Wordist immortals, sometimes thought of as being in the middle of East Sea, sometimes high above in the sky.
* berry: any small, juicy, fleshy fruit, as a strawberry or raspberry.

寄 远

Missing Her Afar

其 一

三鸟别王母，
衔书来见过。
肠断若剪弦，
其如愁思何。
遥知玉窗里，
纤手弄云和。
奏曲有深意，
青松交女萝。
写水山井中，
同泉岂殊波。
秦心与楚恨，
皎皎为谁多。

No. 1

Leaving Queen Mother, three blue birds
Bring down here to me my wife's words.
The letter does my sad mood stir;
How can it quench my thirst for her?
Far there, in the room far away,
My wife her lonely lute does play.
The melody speaks what I mean:
The vine soft clings to the pine green.
The spring does pour into the well;

> From the same source, the flow does swell
> Nostalgia in Ch'in, grief in Ch'u,
> Which is more keen, put on my rue?

* Queen Mother: referring to Mother West, a sovereign goddess living on Mt. Queen in Chinese myths. She was originally described as human-bodied, tiger-toothed, leopard-tailed and hoopoe-haired, regarded as a goddess in charge of women protection, marriage and procreation, and longevity.
* three blue birds: three blue birds by Queen Mother's side, messenger birds in Chinese mythology.
* Ch'in: the Ch'in State or the State of Ch'in (905 B.C.- 206 B.C.), a vassal state, then the first unified regime of China, i.e. the Ch'in Empire.
* Ch'u: a vassal state of Chough, one of the powers in the Warring States period, conquered and annexed by Ch'in in 223 B.C., covering the regions covering present-day Hunan and Hupei and neighboring areas.

其 二

青楼何所在,
乃在碧云中。
宝镜挂秋水,
罗衣轻春风。
新妆坐落日,
怅望金屏空。
念此送短书,
愿同双飞鸿。

No. 2

Where is the blue mansion, o where?
In the white clouds, in the clouds there.
The moon mirrored in the cool stream,
Her dress wind-blown, her smile does beam.
Her new clothes gilt with late sun rays,
At the empty screen she does gaze.
Who is there to send my short words?
I might ask that pair of blue birds.

* the blue mansion: an elegant building painted in blue, sometimes referring to a rich, powerful family.
* screen: a curtain which separates or cuts off, shelters or protects as a light partition, a common image in Chinese literature. A poem in *The Book of Songs* reads like this: "You wait for me before the screen; / Your hat-rings white do tinkle clean, / And your rubies brilliantly sheen."

其 三

本作一行书，
殷勤道相忆。
一行复一行，
满纸情何极。
瑶台有黄鹤，
为报青楼人。
朱颜凋落尽，
白发一何新。
自知未应还，
离居经三春。
桃李今若为，
当窗发光彩。
莫使香风飘，
留与红芳待。

No. 3

A book I intended to write
To quench my thirst, to doff my plight.
One line of love, one line again,
The letter is filled with my pain.
A crane o'er the jade steps does fly,
Which can comfort the one on high.
The rosebud of her face will fade;
Some gray hair grows, with no heed paid.
I can go back yet, which I know,
Though we parted three years ago.
How are plums and peaches today?

By the window brightly they ray!
Do let the fragrance stay, not gone;
May it with the blooms linger on.

* crane: one of a family of large, long-necked, long-legged, heronlike birds allied to the rails, a symbol of integrity and longevity in Chinese culture, only second to the phoenix in cultural importance.
* jade steps: the steps before, and leading to, a palace hall, often used as a metonymy for the court.
* plums and peaches: a metonymy for plants in general; a metaphor for disciples or students.

其 四

玉箸落春镜，
坐愁湖阳水。
闻与阴丽华，
风烟接邻里。
青春已复过，
白日忽相催。
但恐荷花晚，
令人意已摧。
相思不惜梦，
日夜向阳台。

No. 4

To the spring mirror her tear drips;
By the lake she sits, sad her lips.
This lake with Shade Belle's town, I hear,
Is linked in mist, so they are near.
My prime has passed, for ever gone;
The sun does urge me to go on.
Too soon, the lotus blooms will die;
In this wretched state I but sigh.
In my dream now I haste away
To her balcony night and day.

* Shade Belle: referring to Lihua Yin (A.D. 5 – A.D. 64) if transliterated, born into a prominent family, the empress in Lightmight's reign, wife of Emperor Lightmight.
* lotus: any of various waterlilies, especially the white or pink Asian lotus, used as a

religious symbol in Hinduism and Buddhism. The lotus is a common image in Chinese literature, as two lines of a lyric by Hsiu Ouyang (A.D. 1007 - A.D. 1072) read: "A thunder brings rain to the wood and pool, / The rain hushes the lotus, drips cool."

其 五

远忆巫山阳，
花明渌江暖。
踌躇未得往，
泪向南云满。
春风复无情，
吹我梦魂断。
不见眼中人，
天长音信短。

No. 5

I think of Mt. Witch far away,
The river's warm and the flowers gay.
I pace to and fro with a sad frown;
Looking south, I feel tears drip down.
And the vernal wind is perverse,
Which blows my sad dream to disperse.
In fuzziness, I lose sight of her;
The day long, no news, what a blur!

* Mt. Witch: a mythical and religious mountain, which was thought to be a range of mountains in today's Sha'anhsi Province.

其 六

阳台隔楚水，
春草生黄河。
相思无日夜，
浩荡若流波。
流波向海去，
欲见终无因。
遥将一点泪，
远寄如花人。

No. 6

Sun Mound is kept off by the Ch'u;
Spring grass on the Yellow does grow.
Day and night my longings accrue,
Surging, merging, like the east flow.
The water pours into the ocean;
And my love for her stirs a motion.
May I far away send my gloom
To the belle beaming like a bloom!

* Sun Mound: the mound where Goddess of Mt. Witch dated with King Hsiang of Ch'u.
* the Ch'u: the Ch'u River. The Min River joins Lake Cavehall and flows more than 150 kilometers to Land Sand Prefecture, and this part is called the Ch'u River.
* the Yellow: the Yellow River, the second longest river in China, the cradle of Chinese civilization. As legend goes, the river derived from a yellow dragon that, couchant on Midland Plain, ate yellow soil, flooded crops, devoured people and stock, and was finally tamed by Great Worm, the First King of Hsia (cir. 21 B.C.- 16 B.C.). Its fertile valleys were turned into fields of rice, barley and oscillating corn, amid gleaming streams and lakes.

其 七

妾在舂陵东，
君居汉江岛。
一日望花光，
往来成白道。
一为云雨别，
此地生秋草。
秋草秋蛾飞，
相思愁落晖。
何由一相见，
灭烛解罗衣。

No. 7

I live on Pounding Ridge's east side;
On the shoal in the Han you bide.
I look at the spring sites all day;
Coming and going paves the way.
Since I left Mt. Witch's cloud and rain,
I've been lonely, dry grass again.
Dry grass again, butterflies fly;
The afterglow drowns my sad sigh.
When can we meet, from eye to eye?
The lamp off, your dress I untie.

* Pounding Ridge: an ancient town of Han, in today's Dateshine (Tsaoyang) County, Hupei Province.
* the Han: the Han River, a large tributary of the Long River, which originates in today's Shanhsi and flows southwestward through Hupei, joining the main stream in

today's Wuhan.
* Mt. Witch: a mythical and religious mountain, which was thought to be a range of mountains in Sha'anhsi. It alludes to the tryst of Nymph with King Hsiang of Ch'u.
* cloud and rain: King Hsiang of Chu once in his dream saw a nymph whose beauty captivated his heart, and who, on being asked who she was, replied: In the morning I am the cloud and in the evening the rain, and then they had their romance. The king so infatuated pined for the cloud and rain, day in and day out ever after.

其 八

忆昨东园桃李红碧枝，
与君此时初别离。
金瓶落井无消息，
令人行叹复坐思。
坐思行叹成楚越，
春风玉颜畏销歇。
碧窗纷纷下落花，
青楼寂寂空明月。
两不见，
但相思。
空留锦字表心素，
至今缄愁不忍窥。

No. 8

Gone yesterday, in East Garden peach and plum did ray;
That was the time we set off on our way.
Like a gold vase dropped to the well, no news,
As I go with woes, so I sit with rues.
Sitting with rues, going with woes, we sigh;
As spring wind blows to your face, blossoms die.
By your window, the blossoms are in flight;
Your tower is vacant, and the moon is bright.
We two apart,
Sad is our heart.
The letter speaks what's in your heart field,
But I dare not look in and keep it sealed.

* peach and plum: a metonymy for plants in general or a flowering season, often used as a metaphor for disciples or students, and sometimes symbolizing a flashy life.
* in East Garden peach and plum did ray: an allusion to Chi Juan's poem: A trail's made under the trees fine; / East garden sees peach and plum shine.

其 九

长短春草绿,
缘阶如有情。
卷施心独苦,
抽却死还生。
睹物知妾意,
希君种后庭。
闲时当采掇,
念此莫相轻。

No. 9

Long or short there grows spring grass green
Along the steps, like they've love keen.
Cochin grass has a hardy heart;
Heart cut off, again it does start.
Seeing this grass, you know my woe;
In your back yard, may you it sow.
When you're free, you can pick a blade;
Don't forget my heart for you made.

* Cochin grass has a hardy heart; / Heart cut off, again it does start: In Calm Town (Ninghsiang) of today's Hunan Province, there is a lot of cochin grass, which can survive even if one cuts off its heart.

其 十

鲁缟如玉霜，
笔题月氏书。
寄书白鹦鹉，
西海慰离居。
行数虽不多，
字字有委曲。
天末如见之，
开缄泪相续。
泪尽恨转深，
千里同此心。
相思千万里，
一书值千金。

No. 10

On the silken cloth like jade bright,
A letter in Jouchih I'll write.
May the white parrot send it west
To where my man drifts as a guest.
Though there is not many a line,
Each word is an intended sign.
One day this letter if he reads,
His tears will drip like shining beads.
The tears turn into grief so smart;
Tho far away, we've the same heart.
My griefs myriads of miles, behold;
A letter's worth a mound of gold.

* Jouchih: indicating an area around Hohsi Corridor, which is 1,000 kilometers long and about 100 kilometer wide, and the nationality or language bearing the name.
* parrot: the bird that can simulate human laughter and speech, having a hooked bill, paired toes, and usually brilliant plumage; a metaphor for the poet himself in this poem.

其十一

爱君芙蓉婵娟之艳色，
色可餐兮难再得。
怜君冰玉清迥之明心，
情不极兮意已深。
朝共琅玕之绮食，
夜同鸳鸯之锦衾。
恩情婉娈忽为别，
使人莫错乱愁心。
乱愁心，
涕如雪。
寒灯厌梦魂欲绝，
觉来相思生白发。
盈盈汉水若可越，
可惜凌波步罗袜。
美人美人兮归去来，
莫作朝云暮雨兮飞阳台。

No. 11

I love your beauty, a lotus bloom, a moon bright;
Your glamour outshines all scenes, any sight.
I love your virtue, crystalline like precious jade;
Your amour's so deep that will never fade.
For breakfast we've nectar and yummy food;
For the night we share a love quilt and hood.
So deep in love, it's hard to part, to go;
Don't be distressed, not overwhelmed with woe.
Overwhelmed with woe,

Nose streaming with snow.
The cold lamp, my nightmare and my despair!
I waken to find I have grown gray hair.
The brimming Han River I'll wade tho wide;
My socks get wet before I touch the tide.
My lady, my lady, come back soon while you may.
Don't be an even rain dashing to my balcony I pray.

* nectar: in Chinese and Greek mythologies, the drink of the gods or fairies, and in botany, the saccharine substance secreted by some plants and forming the base of natural honey.
* the Han River: the longest large tributary of the Long River, which originates from the Ch'in Ridge in today's Sha'anhsi and flows southwestward through Hupei, joining the main stream at Hankow, one of the most important rivers in China,

长　信　宫

月皎昭阳殿，
霜清长信宫。
天行乘玉辇，
飞燕与君同。
更有欢娱处，
承恩乐未穷。
谁怜团扇妾，
独坐怨秋风？

Long Faith Palace

O'er Sun Glare Palace the moon's bright;
In Long Faith Hall one feels frost bite.
His Majesty in the sedan,
Has Swallow close, like a light swan.
There are more happy hours to spend;
His grace and vim last without end.
Who pities the belle who does sigh?
She sits there, grudging the wind sly.

* Long Faith Palace: the most important building in the palace complex of Long Happiness Palace, usually the residence of an empress dowager.
* Sun Glare Palace: a Han palace where Flying Swallow's sister, Hote Chao, a cosseted lady, used to dwell.
* Swallow: referring to Flying Swallow, Feiyan Chao (45 B.C.- A.D. 1). Starting as a dancer in the residence of Princess Yang'o, she attracted Emperor Complete of Han's attention, hence she was made an imperial concubine and later the empress. As her

sister Hote Chao came and attracted the emperor, Swallow gradually lost the emperor's attention.

* swan: a large web-footed, long-necked bird (subfamily *Cygninae*), allied to but heavier than the goose and noted for its grace on the water, as the whooper, the trumpeter swan, and the whistling swan.

长门怨二首

Plaint in Long Gate Hall, Two Poems

其 一

天回北斗挂西楼，
金屋无人萤火流。
月光欲到长门殿，
别作深宫一段愁。

No.1

The Big Dipper turns to hang o'er West Tower;
No one in Golden House, the fireflies glow.
The moon would on Long Gate Hall her rays shower
To look deep inside for a piece of woe.

* Long Gate Hall: referring to Long Gate Palace, where Petite moved after being deposed. Since then, Long Gate Palace has become a symbol of an estranged queen.
* the Big Dipper, the Dipper: a constellation composed of seven bright stars, which looks like a spoon in the sky.
* Golden House: Lord Martial of Han once loved Petite and promised her a golden house when they were young. But Petite lost his love and moved to Long Gate Palace after being deposed. Now, Golden House is used as a metaphor for any palace or an abode for the fair sex.
* firefly: any of a family (Lampyridae) of winged beetles, active at night, whose abdomens usually glow with a luminescent light.

其 二

桂殿长愁不记春,
黄金四屋起秋尘。
夜悬明镜青天上,
独照长门宫里人。

No. 2

The Hall, full of sorrow, heaves a long sigh;
It knows not spring but sees autumn dust rise.
The bright mirror hangs high in the blue sky
Just for the one that asks the cold room whys.

* the Hall: referring to Long Gate Palace, where Petite moved after being deposed. Since then, Long Gate Palace has become a symbol of an estranged queen, a metonymy for a concubine left alone in it.

春　怨

白马金羁辽海东，
罗帷绣被卧春风。
落月低轩窥烛尽，
飞花入户笑床空。

Plaint in Spring

The harnessed white horse to East Liao does fly;
Silk net, brocade quilt, in spring breeze I lie.
Moonlit, the screen sees the candle off gone.
The bloom flies into the room and laughs: none.

* East Liao: an area east of the Liao River and north of East Sea, about 500 square kilometers.
* screen: a curtain which separates or cuts off, shelters or protects as a light partition, a common image in Chinese literature. Two lines from a Sung lyric by Haowen Yüan reads like this: "The drizzle falls before my tower's sill; / 'Broidered with crabapples, the screen's chill."
* candle: a cylinder of tallow, wax, or other solid fat, containing a wick, to give light when burning, first seen in literature in the Eastern Han dynasty. The most famous lines about candles are from a poem by a T'ang poet named Shangyin Li, "Silkworms stop offering silk when they die; / Candles become ash as their tears run dry."

代 赠 远

妾本洛阳人，
狂夫幽燕客。
渴饮易水波，
由来多感激。
胡马西北驰，
香鬟摇绿丝。
鸣鞭从此去，
逐虏荡边陲。
昔去有好言，
不言久离别。
燕支多美女，
走马轻风雪。
见此不记人，
恩情云雨绝。
啼流玉箸尽，
坐恨金闺切。
织锦作短书，
肠随回文结。
相思欲有寄，
恐君不见察。
焚之扬其灰，
手迹自此灭。

To Whom Afar in My Wife's Voice

I was from Loshine, married here

To a guy who'll guard the frontier.
Thirsty, you drink the Change's splash;
More often than not, you're so rash.
The Hun horse to the northwest neighs
And its green mane in fragrance sways.
You gallop and a whip you crack,
And chase the foes for an attack.
You said you'd return before long;
It's such a delay, wrong, wrong, wrong!
In Mt. Rouge girls like blossoms blow;
And can gallop like whirling snow.
From now you may forget me all,
Like a rain from the clouds does fall.
My tears like jade beads drip and flow;
In this gold room, I'm grabbed by woe.
I write you short verse on brocade,
A palindrome with sadness made.
I'd send it to you in north land,
Afraid you may not understand.
I'll burn it and scatter the ash,
So that it'll be gone in a flash.

* Loshine: Loyang if transliterated, the eastern of the two great cities that served as capitals in the early Chinese dynasties, and second city of the Empire in T'ang times, when it had about 800,000 inhabitants.
* the Change: referring to the River Change, by which Chingk'e bid farewell to his lord and friend, and set off for his mission.
* Mt. Rouge: the Rouge Mountains, a range of mountains in today's Ope-arms (Changyeh), Kansu Province, lush with pines and cypresses and various kinds of plants and grass.

陌上赠美人

骏马骄行踏落花,
垂鞭直拂五云车。
美人一笑褰珠箔,
遥指红楼是妾家。

To the Beauty on the Lane

The horse trots on fallen blossoms, tic-tac;
O'er the five-cloud cart he a whip does crack.
The beauty draws up her pearled screen and smiles:
"That's my tower", as she points to the red tiles.

* the five-cloud cart: the kind of carts for immortals, a metaphor in this poem.
* screen: a curtain or shelter which separates or cuts off, shelters or protects as a light partition, a common image in Chinese literature. A poem in *The Book of Songs* reads like this: "You wait for me before the screen; / Your hat-rings white do tinkle clean, / And your rubies brilliantly sheen."

闺 情

流水去绝国，
浮云辞故关。
水或恋前浦，
云犹归旧山。
恨君流沙去，
弃妾渔阳间。
玉箸夜垂流，
双双落朱颜。
黄鸟坐相悲，
绿杨谁更攀。
织锦心草草，
挑灯泪斑斑。
窥镜不自识，
况乃狂夫还。

A Lady's Rue

The water out of the land pours;
The cloud flies from the pass and soars.
The water loves its former shore;
The cloud floats where it was before.
To go to Quick Sand you've pined,
In Fishshine leaving me behind.
At night my tears drop like jade beads;
The glamour of my face recedes.
The oriole sitting cries: chick, chick.

A willow twig who'll for me pick?
Weaving brocade, I'm in no mood,
In lamplight and in tears like dewed.
Mirrored, I don't know who I am,
Let alone you, a brainless sham.

* Quick Sand: name of a lake, also known as Chüyan Sea, in today's Inner Mongolia, 80 kilometers from Ope-arms, that is, today's Changyeh, Kansu Province.
* Fishshine: Fishshine Prefecture, today's Chi District, Tientsin.
* oriole: golden oriole, one of the family of passerine birds, which looks bright yellow with contrasting black wings and sings beautiful songs.

代 别 情 人

清水本不动，
桃花发岸傍。
桃花弄水色，
波荡摇春光。
我悦子容艳，
子倾我文章。
风吹绿琴去，
曲度紫鸳鸯。
昔作一水鱼，
今成两枝鸟。
哀哀长鸡鸣，
夜夜达五晓。
起折相思树，
归赠知寸心。
覆水不可收，
行云难重寻。
天涯有度鸟，
莫绝瑶华音。

Seeing Off Husband in My Wife's Voice

Like the limpid water you stay;
I'm a peach blooming by the bay.
The peach bloom plays with water hue;
The waves sway spring light to and fro.
I love your glamour, your face bright;

You love my writings, what I write.
The wind blows to my lute I pluck,
Hence the tune of *The Mandarin Duck*.
Happy like fish, we used to play;
Now I'm a bird on a lone spray.
Sad, sad, it cries: coo, coo, woo, woo;
Till night it cries and till dawn, too.
I break a love acacia spray,
To express to you what I'd say.
Spilled wine can't be got to your cup;
A cloud gone you can't follow up.
Howe'er far off, there're migrant birds;
Send me your news, send me your words.

* peach: any of the plant (*Prunus Percica*), bearing a fleshy, juicy, edible drupe, cultivated in many varieties in temperate zones considered sacred in China, often used as a metaphor for a young woman, as a section of a poem in *The Book of Songs* reads: "The peach twigs sway, / Ablaze the flower; / Now she's married away, / Befitting her new bower."
* *The Mandarin Duck*: an ancient tune. Mandarin ducks are used to imply eternal love in Chinese culture because they usually show up in pairs.

代 秋 情

几日相别离,
门前生稆葵。
寒蝉聒梧桐,
日夕长鸣悲。
白露湿萤火,
清霜凌兔丝。
空掩紫罗袂,
长啼无尽时。

Autumn Rue in My Wife's Voice

You left just a few days ago;
Before the door thin mallows grow.
Cicadas in phoenix trees chill
Cry in the day, and at night shrill.
The fireflies are wet with white dew;
The dodders are touched with frost hue.
My silk clothes I might as well doff;
I weep ceaselessly, on and off.

* mallow: a plant of the genus *Malva* with edible leaves, which was one of the five most popular vegetables in ancient China.
* cicada: a homopterous insect that sings its song of summer and shrills in autumn, a symbol of death and resurrection in Chinese culture because of its metamorphosis and recycle. Therefore, in ancient China, a jade cicada figure was put in the mouth of a dead body with such an intention of eternal life.
* firefly: any of a family (Lampyridae) of winged beetles, active at night, whose

abdomens usually glow with a luminescent light.
* dodder: a leafless twining herb of the genus *Cuscuta*, parasitic on several other plants to which it adheres by suckers.

对　　酒

蒲萄酒，金叵罗，
吴姬十五细马驮。
青黛画眉红锦靴，
道字不正娇唱歌。
玳瑁筵中怀里醉，
芙蓉帐底奈君何！

Drinking Wine

Lo, good grape wine, and golden fur;
The girl fifteen, a pony carries her.
Brows painted with indigo and in red shoes;
Not pronouncing well, she sings: O red rose.
At hawksbill feast, drunk, she flies to your chest;
With her in your jade bed, how can you rest?

* grape: any grapevine yielding grapes, smooth-skinned, edible, juicy, berrylike fruit, introduced to China by Chien Chang (164 B.C.- 114 B.C.) in the Han dynasty.
* grape wine: first brewed in Ferghana, introduced to China in the early T'ang dynasty.
* pony: a small horse of any of a number of breeds, usually not over 58 inches, high at the withers.
* rose: any of a genus of shrubs of the rese family, characteristically with prickly stems, alternate compound leaves, and five-parted, usually fragrant flowers of red, pink, white, yellow, etc, having many stamens. It is often used as a metaphor for beauty or love.
* hawksbill feast: a fabulous banquet, which is held for a happy reunion or to celebrate an anniversary in Chinese culture, sometimes also called nectar feast or banquet.

怨　　情

新人如花虽可宠，
故人似玉由来重。
花性飘扬不自持，
玉心皎洁终不移。
故人昔新今尚故，
还见新人有故时。
请看陈后黄金屋，
寂寂珠帘生网丝。

The Plaint

The new wife, like a rosebud, is adored;
The old one, like a diamond, is there stored.
That catkin in flight can't itself contain;
A heart crystalline does so pure remain.
The old were new and the new will be old;
The blaze, ardent, will in the end turn cold.
Lo, Empress Ch'en was a belle rarely seen,
Now spiderweb all over her pearled screen.

* catkin: a deciduous scaly spike of flowers, as in the willow, an image of flippancy in Chinese literature.
* Empress Ch'en: referring to Petite, an empress of Han. When Lord Martial was a child, he loved his cousin, Petite, and promised her a gold house when he grew up. Later Petite became Empress Ch'en but lost Emperor Martial's love and moved to Long Gate Palace after being deposed.
* spiderweb: web constructed by a spider for the capture of prey such as flies and insects.

A spider is a wingless arachnid having an unsegmented abdomen and capable of spinning silk, usually regarded as a mascot in China, a symbol of good luck or good news to come, sometimes also bespeaking desolation, especially in a deserted room.

* screen: a curtain or shelter which separates or cuts off, shelters or protects as a light partition, a common image in Chinese literature. Two lines from a Sung lyric by Haowen Yüan reads like this: "The drizzle falls before my tower's sill; / 'Broidered with crabapples, the screen's chill."

湖边采莲妇

小姑织白纻，
未解将人语。
大嫂采芙蓉，
溪湖千万重。
长兄行不在，
莫使外人逢。
愿学秋胡妇，
贞心比古松。

A Woman Gathering Lotus Pods on the Lake

She weaves ramie cloth, Little Sis;
She does not know what the world is.
Big Sis gathers lotus pods there;
Lake Brook teems with lotuses fair.
Big Brother is out, far away;
With nobody, Sis, you should stay.
May we now learn from Cutewho's wife,
To live a faithful and chaste life.

* ramie: a perennial plant of the nettle family, grown in warm climate for the strong bast fibre of the stem, which is used for making cloth.
* Little Sis: referring to the younger sister-in-law
* Big Sis: referring to the elder sister-in-law.
* Big Brother: referring to Little Sis's elder brother.
* Cutewho: an unfaithful husband from the State of Lu in the Spring and Autumn period, He flirted with a beautiful mulberry gatherer who was actually his own wife, whom he left five days after his wedding and had not seen for five years.

怨　　情

美人卷珠帘，
深坐颦蛾眉。
但见泪痕湿，
不知心恨谁。

The Plaint

The belle rolls up the pearly screen,
Then seated deep, she frowns and stares.
Traces of her tears can be seen;
Against whom is the grudge she bears?

* pearly screen: a curtain decorated with pearls, which separates or cuts off, shelters or protects as a light partition. The curtain is a common image in Chinese literature. As a poem in *The Book of Songs* reads, "You wait for me before the screen; / Your hat-rings white do tinkle clean, / And your rubies brilliantly sheen."
* orangutan: a large anthropoid ape (genus *Pongo* or *Simia*), having brown-reddish hair, brown skin, small ears, doglike teeth, narrow lips, and long arms reaching to the ankles.

代寄情楚词体

君不来兮,
徒蓄怨积思而孤吟。
云阳一去已远,
隔巫山渌水之沉沉。
留馀香兮染绣被,
夜欲寝兮愁人心。
朝驰余马于青楼,
怳若空而夷犹。
浮云深兮不得语,
却惆怅而怀忧。
使青鸟兮衔书,
恨独宿兮伤离居。
何无情而雨绝,
梦虽往而交疏。
横流涕而长嗟,
折芳洲之瑶华。
送飞鸟以极目,
怨夕阳之西斜。
愿为连根同死之秋草,
不作飞空之落花。

A Plaint in My Wife's Voice, in the Style of Ch'u Lyrics

O far away you're gone,
With grudge, spite and rue, I do linger and croon on;

To the cloud balcony you've gone there,

Kept off by Mt. Witch and water in misty air.

Your odor on quilt and pillow remains;

I would fall asleep but suffer all pains.

At dawn gallop to the brothel I would;

Hesitating, I'm in such a bad mood.

The floating clouds thick, we've nowhere to chat;

Disconsolate I am, worried like that.

I'd ask a messenger bird to reach you;

Lonely living I hate, o this I rue.

How ruthless, Heaven, you keep us apart;

Of my man I dream, so sad my heart.

You weep and sigh, crying out of your soul;

I pick a white bloom for you from the shoal.

You see off the bird with your tearful eyes

And complain of the setting sun with sighs.

Like the grass sharing the same root, I'd with you die,

Not to be a bloom fallen from the sky.

---

* Mt. Witch: a mythical and religious mountain, which was thought to be a range of mountains in today's Sha'anhsi Province. It indicates the tryst of Nymph with King Hsiang of Ch'u.

学 古 思 边

衔悲上陇首，
肠断不见君。
流水若有情，
幽哀从此分。
苍茫愁边色，
惆怅落日曛。
山外接远天，
天际复有云。
白雁从中来，
飞鸣苦难闻。
足系一书札，
寄言难离群。
离群心断绝，
十见花成雪。
胡地无春晖，
征人行不归。
相思杳如梦，
珠泪湿罗衣。

Thinking of the Border like Ancients

I walk onto Mt. Bulge, so sad;
You beyond me, I feel like mad.
The water, as if from my heart,
Flows far away, for e'er apart.
The border shrouded in thick haze;

To your camp in twilight I gaze.
Peaks below look to peaks on high;
Endless clouds float out of the sky.
A white wild goose flies here from there;
Its saddened cries I cannot bear.
On its claw his letter is tied,
Full of nostalgia from inside.
From inside is his parting woe;
Flowers seen for ten years are now snow.
There's no spring in the north, alack;
A soldier, you cannot come back!
O nostalgia seems like a dream;
My tears on my blouse in vain gleam.

* Mt. Bulge: a mountain located in the southeast of present-day Kansu Province, 2,928 meters above sea level and about 240 kilometers long from north to south, the borderline between Sha'anhsi Loess Plateau and West Bulge Loess Plateau.
* wild goose: an undomesticated goose that is caring and responsible, taken as a symbol of benevolence, righteousness, good manner, wisdom and faith in Chinese culture.

思　　边

去年何时君别妾？
南园绿草飞蝴蝶。
今岁何时妾忆君，
西山白雪暗秦云。
玉关去此三千里，
欲寄音书那可闻？

Thinking of the Border

Last year, when did you say me good-bye?
The grass in South Park saw butterflies fly.
This year, how often in vain I miss you?
The mountains west in Ch'in are veiled in snow.
Jade Pass is one thousand miles off from here;
I'd send my voice letter, can you e'er hear?

* The grass in South Park saw butterflies fly: an allusion to a Chin Poet Chingyang Chang's line: The butterflies in South Park fly.
* Ch'in: the Ch'in State or the State of Ch'in (905 B.C.- 206 B.C.), enfeoffed as a dependency of Chough by King Piety of Chough in 905 B.C. and enfeoffed as a vassal state by King Peace of Chough in 770 B.C. In the ten years from 230 B.C. to 221 B.C., Ch'in wiped out the other six powers and became the first unified regime of China, i.e. the Ch'in Empire.
* Jade Pass: Jade Gate Pass, built in the Han dynasty, located in the north of today's Tunhuang, Kansu Province. As is recorded, to guard against Hun and Chiang invasions, Emperor Martial of Han formed alliance with other Asian nations in the western regions to initiate a route between east and west, and there he instituted four sires and built two passes with beacons west of the Yellow River. Fortresses were made from Lingchü to Wine Spring in 111 B.C. and more fortresses made from Wine Spring to Jade Gate.

口号吴王美人半醉

风动荷花水殿香，
姑苏台上宴吴王。
西施醉舞娇无力，
笑倚东窗白玉床。

Making Fun of King of Wu's Beauty, Who Is Half Drunk, an Oral Impromptu

Wind stirs the lotus, balm filling the court;
The king on Kusu Mound holds a feast to sport.
The beauty drunk and soft does all beguile;
The jade bed neath East Window likes her smile.

* Kusu Mound: a palace King Futs'ai of Wu built for West Maid, and his weakness for this beautiful woman led to his suicide and the loss of his kingdom.
* the beauty: referring to West Maid who was once a laundry lady in the State of Yüeh, which was then a tributary to the State of Wu. Because of her beauty, West Maid was selected to be trained in Yüeh's palace, and sent to King Futs'ai of Wu as a spy. She quickly won the king's affection, causing him to be indulged in her charm. As a result, the State of Wu waned and perished.

代美人愁镜

Her Sadness in the Mirror

其 一

明明金鹊镜，
了了玉台前。
拂拭皎冰月，
光辉何清圆。
红颜老昨日，
白发多去年。
铅粉坐相误，
照来空凄然。

No. 1

The Golden Crane Mirror so bright
Shines and shines before the steps white.
As dusted, like the moon it beams;
And how crystal and round it gleams!
Her beauty fades to disappear;
Her gray hair is more than last year.
To old cheeks, rouge may be a stain;
Herself mirrored, she sighs in vain.

---

* the Golden Crane Mirror: a mirror that reflects one's chasteness. A husband broke the mirror into halves when he went away from home. He took one half and left the other at home. When his wife had an affair, the half at home turned into a magpie that flew to inform her husband.

* the moon: the celestial body that revolves around the earth from west to east as a satellite, which appears at night and gives off shining silvery light, an image of purity and solitude in Chinese culture.

其 二

美人赠此盘龙之宝镜,
烛我金缕之罗衣。
时将红袖拂明月,
为惜普照之余晖。
影中金鹊飞不灭,
台下青鸾思独绝。
藁砧一别若箭弦,
去有日,来无年。
狂风吹却妾心断,
玉箸并堕菱花前。

No. 2

The belle gives me a mirror with a dragon carved so bold
That sheds light to my clothes of gold.
I hold the mirror up to the moon bright,
And it does reflect the remanent light.
Gold Magpie on the edge flies not away;
Blue Phoenix neath the sad table does stay.
The cutting board is like an arrow gone;
What is gone is gone, and it won't come on.
A wild zephyr blows my heart to break down;
My tears will all the water chestnuts drown.

* dragon: a fabulous serpent-like giant winged animal that can change its girth and length, a totem of the Chinese nation, a symbol of benevolence and sovereignty in Chinese culture.
* Golden Magpie: name of a mirror that reflects one's chasteness. A husband broke the

mirror into halves when he left home. He took one half and left the other at home. When his wife had an affair, the half at home turned into a magpie and flew to inform the husband.
* Blue Phoenix: a magical creature kept by Queen Mother in Chinese mythology.
* water chestnut: the hard horned edible fruit of an aquatic plant.

赠 段 七 娘

罗袜凌波生网尘，
那能得计访情亲？
千杯绿酒何辞醉？
一面红妆恼杀人。

To Tuan, Sis Seven

You, like Nymph, walk on tiptoe, stirring dust;
Can you come close, closer, to quench my lust?
Drink one thousand cups! How can I drunk be?
How blessed, your beguiling eyes annoy me!

* Nymph: a beautiful fairy dwelling at Mt. Witch, who shaped herself as clouds at dawn and turned into rain at dusk. King Huai of Chu once saw her in his dream was captivated by her beauty, and then they had their romance. The king so infatuated pined for the cloud and rain, day in and day out ever after.

别内赴征三首

Farewell to My Wife to Join the Army, Three Poems

其 一

王命三征去未还，
明朝离别出吴关。
白玉高楼看不见，
相思须上望夫山。

No. 1

Recruited three times, I'm leaving at last;
Tomorrow, we'll go thru Wu Pass so fast.
On White Jade Tower you will see me no more;
Climb up Mt. O-Come-Hubby that does soar.

* Wu Pass: referring to Wu's border, the location unidentified. Wu, as a name, originated from the State of Wu, one of the Five Hegemons in the Spring and Autumn period, which developed into Three Wu's in the Han dynasty: Wu Shire (Wuchün), Wu Rise (Wuhsing) and Wu Summit (Wuhui), covering today's South Chiangsu, North Chechiang and South Anhui.
* Mt. O-Come-Hubby: located in Shantung. A husband of Ch'i was summoned to hard work only three days after his wedding. Year in, year out, the wife climbed high to wait for her husband and finally turned into a rock standing firmly on top of the mountain. More than one hill in China has taken this name because of a similar case of a wife who climbed the height to watch for the return of her husband.

其 二

出门妻子强牵衣，
问我西行几日归？
归时倘佩黄金印，
莫学苏秦不下机。

No. 2

When I go out, you pull my coat and vest,
And ask me: When will you return from west?
If I returned with Premier Su's gold seal,
Would you regard my feat as a vain deal?

* Premier Su: Ch'in Su (? -284 B.C.), a political strategist in the Warring States period. When he succeeded, it occurred to him that if he had a farmland at early age, he would not have been a premier. When young, he went out, seeking for a career, but returned in rags and tatters. His wife would not take the trouble of leaving her place at the loom to greet him. However, he succeeded later in his scheme of the federation of six weaker states against the strong state of Ch'in, and he was appointed premier with a gold seal from each of the six states thus combined.

* gold seal: In ancient China, the seal for a premier, a general or prefect was a gold one.

其 三

翡翠为楼金作梯,
谁人独宿倚门啼?
夜坐寒灯连晓月,
行行泪尽楚关西。

No. 3

We live in our jadeite house with gold stairs;
Who would lean on the door, grabbed by despairs?
You'll sit with the lone lamp till dawn, alas!
String upon string of tears west of Ch'u Pass!

* Ch'u Pass: referring to Ch'u's border, the location unidentified.

秋 浦 寄 内

我今寻阳去，
辞家千里馀。
结荷倦水宿，
却寄大雷书。
虽不同辛苦，
怆离各自居。
我自入秋浦，
三年北信疏。
红颜愁落尽，
白发不能除。
有客自梁苑，
手携五色鱼。
开鱼得锦字，
归问我何如？
江山虽道阻，
意合不为殊。

To My Wife in Autumn Shoal

I left Bankshine early today;
Now I'm three hundred miles away.
By the pond where lotuses blow,
I send a Bolt-letter to you.
Although we suffer different pains,
Divided, our same grief remains.
Since I came to Autumn Shore here,

No news from north many a year.
My prime of life has gone away;
I can't get rid of my hair gray.
A guest has now come from Park Beam,
Carried in hand a five-hued bream.
The fish opend, a letter I find;
You asked what my plan was in mind.
Although we're barred and far away,
In each other we wish to stay.

* Bankshine: an ancient name of present-day Chiuchiang, Chianghsi Province.
* Bolt-letter: a letter expected to reach the receiver soon. Bolt was an old garrison stationed in the Chin dynasty, in today's River Gazer (Wangchiang) County, Anhui Province.
* Autumn Shore: southwest of today's Kuich'ih County, Anhui Province, rich in silver and copper resources and teeming in fauna and flora.
* Park Beam: referring to Liang's Park if transliterated, a royal park built in the capital of Liang in the Western Han dynasty.
* five-hued: of various colors. In Chinese culture, five major colors include blue, red, white, black and yellow.

自 代 内 赠

宝刀截流水，
无有断绝时。
妾意逐君行，
缠绵亦如之。
别来门前草，
秋巷春转碧。
扫尽更还生，
萋萋满行迹。
鸣凤始相得，
雄惊雌各飞。
游云落何山？
一往不见归。
估客发大楼，
知君在秋浦。
梁苑空锦衾，
阳台梦行雨。
妾家三作相，
失势去西秦。
犹有旧歌管，
凄清闻四邻。
曲度入紫云，
啼无眼中人。
女弟争笑弄，
悲羞泪盈巾。
妾似井底桃，
开花向谁笑？
君如天上月，

不肯一回照。
窥镜不自识,
别多憔悴深。
安得秦吉了,
为人道寸心。

A Gift in My Wife's Voice

With your sword the current you chop;
Not at all can you the flow stop.
My mind and heart following you,
Attached, lingering, are like so.
We parted then in autumn keen;
The dry grass by the door turns green.
More grows if you sweep it away,
Lush, so lush, it spreads on the way.
The phoenixes each to each cry;
Male and female, apart they fly.
Like clouds to which mount will they light?
Once gone off, they are out of sight.
A merchant from Great Tower told me:
In Autumn Shore you seem to be.
Park Beam sees me lie neath brocade;
A rain does wash the balustrade.
Three premiers are out of house mine;
We've left West Ch'in as we decline.
I have a pipe left from before;
The clear tune wakens the next door.
The melody rings in the sky;
Sad, there's no beauty in my eye.

At me sisters contend to sneer;
I'm torn between shyness and tear.
Like a peach in the well, I'm low;
To whom can I giggle and blow?
You are like the moon in the sky;
You will never cast back an eye.
The mirror reflects my strange eyes;
How gaunt, how sad, what a surprise!
Where can I have a grackle smart
So that it can express my heart?

* Phoenix: In Chinese myths, phoenixes, auspicious birds, unlike ordinary ones, only perch on parasol trees, and only eat bamboo shoots and pearly stone.
* Great Tower: Mt. Great Tower, a mountain south of Poolton (Ch'ihchow) in today's Anhui Province.
* Autumn Shore: southwest of today's Kuich'ih County, Anhui Province, rich in natural and cultural resources.
* Park Beam: referring to Liang's Park if transliterated, a royal park built in the capital of Liang in the Western Han dynasty.
* West Ch'in: one of the Sixteen Kingdoms (A.D. 304 – A.D. 439), founded by Kuojen Ch'ifu (? – A.D. 388), a Sienpi chieftain.
* grackle: a starling like bird, usually shining and sable-black with a yellow stripe around the neck, which can imitate human speech and singing.

秋浦感主人归燕寄内

霜凋楚关木，
始知杀气严。
寥寥金天廓，
婉婉绿红潜。
胡燕别主人，
双双语前檐。
三飞四回顾，
欲去复相瞻。
岂不恋华屋，
终然谢珠帘。
我不及此鸟，
远行岁已淹。
寄书道中叹，
泪下不能缄。

Sending My Wife a Letter When Moved by the Leaving Swallow from My Host's House in Autumn Shore

Frost freezes the trees at Ch'u Pass,
The killing air proves cruel, alas.
The autumn sky is wide and broad;
Red and green fade with vigor stored.
The swallows to their host says bye;
Both of them beneath the eaves cry.
They fly up and down, to and fro;

Now they glance back: It's hard to go.
Don't they love the beam, clinging fast?
They leave from the pearled screen at last.
Unlike the birds, not a good one,
More than one year afar I've run.
To send her message, sad I feel;
So choked, the letter I can't seal.

* Ch'u Pass: referring to the border of Ch'u.
* pearled screen: a curtain decorated with pearls, which serves to separate or cut off, shelter or protect as a light partition. The curtain is a common image in Chinese literature. A poem in *The Book of Songs* reads like this: "You wait for me before the screen; / Your hat-rings white do tinkle clean, / And your rubies brilliantly sheen."

送内寻庐山女道士李腾空二首

Sending My Wife to Look for Miss Leap-to-Soar, a Woman Hermit in Mt. Lodge, Two Poems

其 一

君寻腾空子，
应到碧山家。
水舂云母碓，
风扫石楠花。
若爱幽居好，
相邀弄紫霞。

No. 1

Miss Leap-to-Soar if you will seek,
Go to the hills, go to the peak.
There the water rams the mica;
Here the zephyr sweeps the heather.
If you'd really live in quietude;
You'd play at clouded altitude.

---

* Mt. Lodge: a famous mountain with historic, cultural and religious attractions, an especially sacred place to Wordists, about 5,000 feet high, in present-day Chianghsi Province.
* Miss Leap-to-Soar: Premier Linfu Li's daughter in the T'ang dynasty. Highborn but keen on the Word, this lady became a Wordist and often gave medical treatments to the people.
* mica: a mineral called silicate in various shapes and hues, having natural veins or lines like a painting, which may be colorless, jet-black, transparent or translucent.

其 二

多君相门女，
学道爱神仙。
素手掬青霭，
罗衣曳紫烟。
一往屏风叠，
乘鸾著玉鞭。

No. 2

A premier's daughter, you are praised;
You learn the Word to be so chaste.
Your fair palms hold up green haze;
Your silk robe tugs at purple rays.
You proceed to Screens Overlay;
You spur the phoenix on your way.

* the Word: referring to Tao if transliterated, the most significant and profoundest concept in Chinese philosophy, which can be identified with the Word or the Logos in the west as they can be seen as one in different clothes, as there is an enormous amount of common ground in the two cosmologies and the doctrines concerning the most fundamental matters such as "the Word is the One" and "God is the One", and the personalization of Being, the progenitor of finite spirits, which are subordinate kinds of Being or merely appearances of the Divine, the One.
* Screens Overlay: nine peaks overlaid on Mt. Lodge.
* phoenix: In Chinese myths, phoenixes, auspicious birds, unlike ordinary ones, only perch on parasol trees, and only eat bamboo shoots and pearly stone.

赠　　内

三百六十日，
日日醉如泥。
虽为李白妇，
何异太常妻。

To My Wife

Three hundred sixty to a day,
So sorry, drunk like mud I stay.
Although you are Pai Li's for life,
Aren't you like Ever the sot's wife?

* Ever: a position in charge of sacrificing rites or a title for the official who during his term of office was responsible for the ritual purification of the Shrine of Imperial Ancestors, his own life being required to be one of monastic purity during his term. There was one named Ever in the Eastern Han dynasty who was strict with himself. When he was seriously ill, his wife came to visit him in the hall of abstinence. Ever burst into rage and sent his wife to jail for he thought her blunder dishonored the deities. People sneered at his stubbornness, so they called him abstinence-holic.

在浔阳非所寄内

闻难知恸哭，
行啼入府中。
多君同蔡琰，
流泪请曹公。
知登吴章岭，
昔与死无分。
崎岖行石道，
外折入青云。
相见若悲叹，
哀声那可闻？

A Letter to My Wife When I'm Jailed in Bankshine

You'd cry if knowing I'm in jail;
To the magistrate you will wail.
Like then Ts'ai to Ts'ao did appeal;
You would ask for a pardon real.
When you climbed the mountain I know,
You almost died of wretched woe.
The small zigzagging path of stone
Rolls up as if to the sky thrown.
Our encounter is one of sighs;
I cannot bear to hear your cries.

* Bankshine: an ancient name of present-day Chiuchiang, Chianghsi Province.

* Ts'ai: referring to Yan Ts'ai (A.D. 174 - A.D. 239), a renowned talented female in the Eastern Han dynasty, good at literature, music and calligraphy. When her husband Tung Ssu was sentenced to death, she came to visit Ts'ao Ts'ao, bare-footed, hair loosened, crying for mercy. Moved by her words, Ts'ao released her husband.
* Ts'ao: referring to Ts'ao Ts'ao (A.D. 155 - A.D. 220), a super lord, the founder of Way in the Three Kingdoms period, crowned as Emperor Martial of Way posthumously.

南流夜郎寄内

夜郎天外怨离居，
明月楼中音信疏。
北雁春归看欲尽，
南来不得豫章书。

A Letter to My Wife While I'm Exiled South in Nightboy

Exiled in Nightboy I bear pain and sour,
With few messages from your moonlit tower.
The northern wild geese will all disappear;
From south no surrogate letter comes here.

* Nightboy: once the biggest kingdom founded by southern barbarians in the southwest existing about three hundred years, from the Warring States period to the Han dynasty. When a Han envoy visited Nigthboy, the king asked: "Which is bigger, Nigthboy or Han?" This self-important question has been a laughing stock ever since. In 27 B.C., Nightboy was wiped out by Han and was made a county.
* wild goose: an undomesticated goose that is caring and responsible, taken as a symbol of benevolence, righteousness, good manner, wisdom and faith in Chinese culture.

越女词五首

Five Lyrics on the Yüeh Girl

其 一

长干吴儿女，
眉目艳新月。
屐上足如霜，
不著鸦头袜。

No. 1

From Long Vale is the Yüeh girl fine;
Her raised brows the crescent outshine.
Her feet in clogs look like frost fair,
For no crow-head socks does she wear.

* Long Vale: a settlement of boatmen, located in Gold Hill, present-day Nanking.
* Yüeh: from the State of Yüeh.
* the crescent: the new moon, which looks just like a girl's brow.
* clog: a wooden soled shoe, an inkling of country life.

其 二

吴儿多白皙，
好为荡舟剧。
卖眼掷春心，
折花调行客。

No. 2

Wu girls look white as if to ray;
They take to boat swinging play.
They give you ogles for romance
And pick a bloom to you entrance.

* Wu girls: southern girls, usually delicate in contrast with shrewish northern girls.

其 三

耶溪采莲女，
见客棹歌回。
笑入荷花去，
佯羞不出来。

No. 3

The lotus girls on the Yeh Stream,
Seeing me, oar back with a beam.
To enter the blossoms they vie,
Pretending to hide and look shy.

* the lotus girls: girls gathering lotus pods.
* the Yeh Stream: or the Joyeh Stream, a stream in the south of present-day Shaohsing, flowing into Lake Mirror. It is said that West Maid did her laundry here.

其 四

东阳素足女，
会稽素舸郎。
相看月未堕，
白地断肝肠。

No. 4

Eastshine sees a lass with feet bare;
Summit sees a lad row to flare.
Both look up at the fading moon;
All in vain, so sadly they croon.

* Eastshine: referring to Tungyang if transliterated, a town in present-day Chechiang.
* Summit: referring to the K'uaichi Mountains in present-day Chechiang Province, where Worm convened a summit attended by vassal lords, hence the name.

其 五

镜湖水如月，
耶溪女如雪。
新妆荡新波，
光景两奇绝。

No. 5

Lake Mirror is like the moon bright;
The Yeh Stream girl is like snow white.
The ripples would lick her dress new;
Wave and light make a magic view.

* Lake Mirror: a large reservoir built in the Han dynasty, higher than the fields and the fields higher than the sea, 310 li in circumference.
* the Yeh Stream: the Joyeh Stream formally, a stream in the south of present-day Shaohsing. It is said that West Maid used to do her laundry here.

浣纱石上女

玉面耶溪女,
青娥红粉妆。
一双金齿屐,
两足白如霜。

The Lass on the Yarn Washing Stone

Bright is the lass in the Yeh Stream;
Black her hair, her rouged face does beam.
Clogs with golden teeth does she wear;
Her feet frost white, she shows a pair.

* the Yeh Stream: or the Joyeh Stream, where West Maid used to do her laundry, a stream in the south of present-day Shaohsing, Chechiang Province.
* clog: a wooden soled shoe, worn casually in summer, an inkling of country life.

示金陵子

金陵城东谁家子，
窃听琴声碧窗里。
落花一片天上来，
随人直度西江水。
楚歌吴语娇不成，
似能未能最有情。
谢公正要东山妓，
携手林泉处处行。

To the Courtesan in Gold Hill

Whose daughter's she in East End of Gold Hill,
Who harks to the lute tune flown to her sill.
She, like a rosebud dropped out of the sky,
Comes 'cross the river west with someone by.
So cute, her soft gait, swift tongue and sweet voice;
So charmed, our yearning, burning and stirred joys.
Lord Glee would ask this belle from the East Hills
To stroll hand in hand through the woods and rills.

* courtesan: a professional woman singer or lutenist, like *geisha* in Japan. In Chinese blue brothel culture, Chinese scholars and officials often visited blue brothels for literary or art recreational activities with a specific courtesan, who was good at singing, dancing and traditional Chinese arts such as zither playing, go playing, calligraphy and painting.
* Gold Hill: referring to Nanking, one of the most well-known ancient capitals in China.
* Lord Glee: Lingyün Hsieh (A.D. 385 – A.D. 433), a highborn poet, idyllist, Buddhist

and traveler, famous for landscape poems. He inherited the title Lord Glee from his grandfather, Hsuan Hsieh (A.D. 343 - A.D. 388), a famous general of Eastern Chin.

* The East Hills: located in Shaohsing, a place for reclusion, where An Hsieh (A.D. 320 - A.D. 385), a general and scholar, used to live.

出妓金陵子呈卢六四首

A Singing Girl in Gold Hill, to Lu Six, Four Poems

其 一

安石东山三十春，
傲然携妓出风尘。
楼中见我金陵子，
何似阳台云雨人？

No. 1

For thirty years at Mt. East, Lord Hsieh stayed;
He toured the world with this singer, called maid.
Have you seen my singer in this high tower?
Is she like Nymph at Mt. Witch in a shower?

* Gold Hill: referring to Nanking, one of the most well-known ancient capitals in China.
* Mt. East: the East Hills, a place Lord Hsieh once lived in reclusion.
* Lord Hsieh: referring to An Hsieh (A.D. 320 – A.D. 385), a statesman and renowned scholar in the Eastern Chin dynasty. When he lived in seclusion at East Hills, he liked traveling among the hills and woods with singing girls.
* Nymph at Mt. Witch: referring to Goddess of Mt. Witch, a beautiful fairy dwelling on Mt. Witch, who shaped herself as clouds at dawn and turned into rain at dusk. In myths, King Huai of Ch'u once met her in his dream, and had an intercourse overnight. The story was recorded by Jade Sung, a student of Yüan Ch'ü's, when he travelled to Cloud Dream Moor with King Hsiang.
* Mt. Witch: a mythical and religious mountain, which was thought to be a range of mountains in Sha'anhsi.

其 二

南国新丰酒，
东山小妓歌。
对君君不乐，
花月奈愁何！

No. 2

From South Clime we have Newrich wine;
From th' East Hills there's a singer fine.
If you're not pleased, what can we do?
E'en blooms and the moon can't help you.

* Newrich: a county, in today's Lintung County, Sha'anhsi Province, well known for its good wine. The county was built by Pang Liu in imitation of his hometown Rich County. Pang Liu, Emperor Highsire, born in Rich, rose from grassroots, wiped out Hsiang's army and established Han, with Long Peace as its capital. As his father missed the beauty and wine of his hometown, Pang Liu made a copy of his hometown and moved the best brewers here, and ever since then Newrich wine has been well-known, attracting generations of litterateurs to sing praise of it.
* The East Hills: located in today's Shaohsing, Chechiang Province, a place for reclusion, where An Hsieh (A.D. 320 – A.D. 385), a general and scholar, used to live. It is often used as a metaphor for a hermitage.

其 三

东道烟霞主，
西江诗酒筵。
相逢不觉醉，
日堕历阳川。

No. 3

You host the Wordists from the east,
And the poets from the west you feast.
We meet, drink but do not feel drunk
Till to the Sun Stream the sun's sunk.

* Wordists: those who believe in and practice the Wordism, naturalist doctrines advanced and elaborated by Laocius (571 B.C.- 471 B.C.). In the T'ang dynasty, an age of proselytism, while Confucianism remained the guiding principle of state and social morality, Wordism had gathered an incrustation of mythology and superstition and was fast winning a following of both the court and the common people. Laocius, the founder, was claimed by the reigning dynasty as its remote progenitor and was honored with an imperial title, Emperor Dark One.
* the Sun Stream: a river in today's Leeshine (Liyang), Anhui Province.

其 四

小妓金陵歌楚声，
家僮丹砂学凤鸣。
我亦为君饮清酒，
君心不肯向人倾。

No. 4

The singer sings a Ch'u tune in Gold Hill;
My boy servant mimics a phoenix trill.
I also drink for you an o'erfilled cup,
But before people why don't you cheer up?

* Gold Hill: referring to Nanking, one of the most well-known ancient capitals in China, second only to Long Peace, that is, today's Hsi-an.
* a Ch'u tune: eclectic, suiting all tastes, high-brow or countrified.
* Phoenix: In Chinese myths, phoenixes, auspicious birds, unlike ordinary ones, only perch on parasol trees, and only eat bamboo shoots and pearly stone.

巴 女 词

巴水急如箭，
巴船去若飞。
十月三千里，
郎行几岁归。

Words of a Wife from Pa

The Pa pours like an arrow starts;
The Pa boat, as if flying, darts.
One thousand miles ten months, alack,
Now leaving, when can you come back?

* the Pa: the Pa River, one of the five rivers in remote or barbaric regions while Pa is an ancient name for the eastern lands of present-day Ssuch'uan.

哭晁卿衡

日本晁卿辞帝都，
征帆一片绕蓬壶。
明月不归沉碧海，
白云愁色满苍梧。

Mourning Heng Ch'ao, a Japanese Friend

To Capital our Japanese friend says bye;
His sail will turn around Fairy Isles high.
The brightness of the moon sinks to the blue;
The pale clouds shroud all mountains with their rue.

* Capital: Long Peace or Ch'ang'an if transliterated, the capital of the T'ang Empire, a cosmopolis with 1,000,000 inhabitants, the largest walled city ever built by man, the center of world religions, Buddhism, Confucianism, Wordism, Nestorianism, Zoroastrianism, and even Islamism represented by Saracens, and the center of education—There were colleges of various grades and special institutes for calligraphy, arithmetic, music, astronomy and so on.
* Heng Ch'ao: Heng Ch'ao (A.D. 698 - A.D. 770), an overseas student from Japan, Abe Nakamaro by his original name. He came to China for education in A.D. 717, and having survived the shipwreck on his trip back to Japan, he served as a high-ranking official in T'ang, first made Protector-General of Tonkin and then Vice-president of the Censorate, a post he held until his death in A.D. 770. When he went back to Japan, the ship sank, and people thought he had drowned in that shipwreck. Hearing the rumour, Pai Li wrote this poem.
* Fairy Isles: an imaginary place on the sea, where fairies dwell.

自溧水道哭王炎

Mourning Yan Wang in the Town of Li River

其 一

白杨双行行，
白马悲路傍。
晨兴见晓月，
更似发云阳。
溧水通吴关，
逝川去未央。
故人万化尽，
闭骨茅山冈。
天上坠玉棺，
泉中掩龙章。
名飞日月上，
义与风云翔。
逸气竟莫展，
英图俄夭伤。
楚国一老人，
来嗟龚胜亡。
有言不可道，
雪泣忆兰芳。

No. 1

The white poplars stand line by line;
The white horse by roadside does whine.
The morning moon gleams to my eyes,

As if from Cloudshine it does rise.
The Li River through Wu Pass flows,
And never turns back while it goes.
My friend is now ash underground,
With bones buried neath a thatch mound.
Heaven's dropped a coffin of jade,
With dragon-figured clothing made.
Your name outshines the moon and sun;
Your virtues wind and cloud outrun.
You have not yet fulfilled your aim;
The netherworld sways all the same.
I, from Ch'u, a man old and worn,
Have come to you and will you mourn.
But I could not myself express;
I wail the orchid, ne'er the less!

* the Town of Li River: a town in today's Hsuan, Anhui Province.
* poplar: any of a genus (*Populus*) of dioecious trees and bushes of the willow family, widely distributed in the northern hemisphere.
* Cloudshine: referring to Yünyang if transliterated, a county in present-day Double Gain (Ch'ungch'ing).
* thatch: any of tall, coarse grasses (genus *Spatina*) widely distributed in temperate zones.
* Heaven's dropped a coffin of jade: Ch'iao Wang, a magistrate in the Han dynasty, went to the capital to visit the emperor half a month. The emperor felt strange to see him so frequently that he ordered a grand scribe to observe Wang privately. The grand scribe found that every time Wang arrived, there would come a pair of wild ducks. When the wild ducks had been captured, they could only find a pair of shoes. Afterwards, there was a jade coffin dropped from the sky, and Wang thought it was Heaven's call, so he got in. As he got in, the coffin closed by itself, and as the coffin was put into the grave, it buried itself.
* orchid: any of a widely distributed family of terrestrial or epiphytic monocotyledonous plants having thickened bulbous roots and often very showy distinctive flowers, one of the four most important floral images in Chinese literature, which are wintersweet, orchid, bamboo and chrysanthemum.

其 二

王公希代宝，
弃世一何早，
吊死不及哀，
殡宫已秋草。
悲来欲脱剑，
挂向何枝好？
哭向茅山虽未摧，
一生泪尽丹阳道。

No. 2

Wang, you're a treasure rare all say,
But all too soon you passed away!
Your funeral I could not attend;
On your tomb cold grass does extend.
So sad, I'd doff my sword for you;
But to hang it, which branch could do?
Tho I can't cry to death by the thatch mound,
On my way to Redshine I'm in tears drowned.

* thatch: any of tall, coarse, thin grasses (genus *Spatina*) widely distributed in temperate zones.
* Redshine: Redshine County, in present-day Chiangsu Province, a county instituted by Emperor First in 221 B.C. and its long history has left us a long list of celebrities and rich legacies.

其 三

王家碧瑶树，
一树忽先摧。
海内故人泣，
天涯吊鹤来。
未成霖雨用，
先失济川材。
一罢广陵散，
鸣琴更不开。

No. 3

Wang, my friend, you're an emerald tree,
A tree that sudd'nly cease to be.
Friends all o'er the world cry in pain,
And out of the sky comes a crane.
This tree has not been put to use;
The world does the great timber lose.
Now for you *Broadridge* I will play,
Then I will hide the lute, oh, nay.

* crane: one of a family of large, long-necked, long-legged, heronlike birds allied to the rails, a symbol of integrity and longevity in Chinese culture, only second to the phoenix in cultural importance.
* *Broadridge*: one of the Ten Tunes in Chinese history.

哭宣城善酿纪叟

纪叟黄泉里，
还应酿老春。
夜台无晓日，
沽酒与何人？

Mourning Old Chi, a Good Brewer in Hsuan

In Hades now you fare;
As e'er Old Spring you brew.
It's night, no dawning there;
Whom do you sell wine to?

* Hades: the abode of the dead, and a euphemism for hell.
* Hsuan: an ancient town in present-day Hsuan, Anhui Province, a county instituted in the early years of the Ch'in Emperor under the Prefecture of Redshine. It became a prefecture in A.D. 281 during the Chin dynasty. It is well known for rich historical legacies, and best remembered for its high-quality rice paper.
* Old Spring: a kind of wine, famous for its good quality.

宣城哭蒋徵君华

敬亭埋玉树，
知是蒋徵君。
安得相如草，
空馀封禅文。
池台空有月，
词赋旧凌云。
独挂延陵剑，
千秋在古坟。

Wailing Hua Chiang the Recruit in Hsuan

Neath Chingt'ing buried a jade tree,
It's you, Hua Chiang, who's died to be.
Where can we Hsiangju's writing gain?
His *Worshiping Verse* rests in vain!
The moon o'er the mound none will view;
Who can understand your book? Few!
Only my sword is hung in gloom,
For e'er to company your tomb!

* Hua Chiang: Pai Li's friend, buried under Mt. Chingt'ing.
* Hsuan: an ancient town in present-day Hsuan, Anhui Province.
* Chingt'ing: an offset of Mt. Yellow, consisting of 60 peaks, rolling more than three miles and 317 meters above sea level, a mountain with many literary legacies.
* Hsiangju: referring to Hsiangju Ssuma (179 B.C. - 118 B.C.) in full name, a representative verse writer in Chinese literary history. He and his wife, Wenchün, a

brilliant woman poet, were equally famous in Chinese history.
* *Worshiping Verse*: a verse that Hsiangju Ssuma wrote to admonish Lord Martial of Han.

拾遗六十四首

Gleanings, 64 Poems

杂言用投丹阳知己兼奉宣慰判官

客从昆仑来，
遗我双玉璞。
云是古之得道者西王母食之馀，
食之可以凌太虚。
受之颇谓绝今昔，
求识江淮人犹乎比石。
如今虽在卞和手，
□□正憔悴，
了了知之亦何益。
恭闻士有调相如，
始从镐京还，
复欲镐京去。
能上秦王殿，
何时回光一相眄。
欲投君，保君年，
幸君持取无弃捐。
无弃捐，服之与君俱神仙。

A Few Words to My Friend in Redshine, an Assistant Official for Publicity

You come all the way from Mt. Queen
And give me a pair of jade crude,
Saying it's something from what Mother West, the immortal, left over from her food.
Eating it, one can to the great void soar;

Owning it, one transcends now and before.
Inquired about it, one from South Land compares it to ore.
What's a real treasure is with Ho Pien,
Who was so wronged;
What's the use of it, known a bit, no more?
You've been given a proper post, I hear.
You've come here from the capital
And to the capital you'll go from here.
Levees at court you can attend;
When will you come and to me condescend?
I would go to the court, and there serve the lord.
May His Majesty never me despise,
Never me despise, so that the lord and I would like gods rise.

* Redshine: Redshine County, in present-day Chiangsu Province, a county instituted by Emperor First in 221 B.C. and its long history has left us a long list of celebrities and rich legacies.
* Mt. Queen: Mt. Kunlun if transliterated, the most sacred mountain in China. It starts from the Eastern Pamir Plateau, stretches across New Land (Hsinchiang) and Tibet, and extends to Blue Sea (Ch'inghai), with an average altitude of 5,500 – 6,000 meters. In Chinese myths, Mt. Queen is where Mother West dwells.
* Mother West: a sovereign goddess living on Mt. Queen in Chinese myths. She was originally described as human-bodied, tiger-toothed, leopard-tailed and hoopoe-haired, regarded as a goddess in charge of women protection, marriage and procreation, and longevity.
* Ho Pien: from Ch'u in the Spring and Autumn period. He failed twice and lost his legs in an attempt to present his crude jade to monarchs of Ch'u before Lord Civil of Ch'u's enthronement. Ho held the jade stone crying bitterly for the previous misjudgment. Up to this point, the precious jade was finally appreciated by the new lord.
* levee: a morning reception or an assembly at the court of a sovereign or at the house of a great personage. In ancient China, a levee at court was held every five days.

南陵五松山别荀七

六即颍水荀，
何惭许郡宾。
相逢太史奏，
应是聚贤人。
玉隐且在石，
兰枯还见春。
俄成万里别，
立德贵清真。

Farewell to Hsun Seven at Mt. Five Pines in Southridge

You're like Hsun on the River Ying;
In front of Ch'en you don't feel shy.
Our encounter is a great thing!
As Tsou said, it's saints that come by.
Jade hidden looms in a rock pile;
Orchids rotten the spring will see.
Soon we'll part, so many a mile;
May you virtuous and simple be.

* Southridge: Southridge County in today's Anhui Province, a gateway to Two Mountains and One Lake (Mt. Yellow, Mt. Nine Flowers, and Great Peace Lake), established as a county in A.D. 525 by Emperor Martial of Liang (A.D. 464 - A.D. 549) in the Southern Dynasties period.
* Mt. Five Pines: located in today's T'ungling, Anhui Province, so named because there grew five pines on the very top. According to *Geographical Wonders* compiled in the

Southern Sung dynasty, "The mountain boasted old pines, five in one, a pentad, reaching high to the sky with scale-like bark on the trunk."
* Hsun: referring to Shu Hsun, a minister of high reputation in the Eastern Han dynasty.
* the River Ying: the first and largest branch of the Huai River, originating from Mt. Tower.
* Ch'en: referring to Shih Ch'en (A.D. 104 – A.D. 187), an official from Yingshade south of the Ying River in the Eastern Han dynasty.
* orchid: a monocotyledonous plant having thickened bulbous roots and often very showy distinctive flowers, one of the four most important floral images in Chinese literature, which are wintersweet, orchid, bamboo and chrysanthemum.

观 鱼 潭

观鱼碧潭上，
木落潭水清。
日暮紫鳞跃，
圆波处处生。
凉烟浮竹尽，
秋月照沙明。
何必沧浪去，
兹焉可濯缨。

Watching Fish in a Pondlet

I watch fish by the pondlet green;
Leaves fall onto the water clean.
The dusk dyes the fish that out leap
And whirling ripples they can reap.
Cool mist thins out from the bamboo;
Autumn Luna does the sand woo.
Why retreat to hills, why should you?
You can wash your sash with the blue.

* bamboo: a tall, tree-like or shrubby grass in tropical and semi-tropical regions, a symbol of integrity and altitude, one of the four most important botanical images in Chinese literature, which are wintersweet, orchid, bamboo and chrysanthemum. Bamboo shoots, fresh or dried, are widely used in Chinese cuisine, bamboo rats and bamboo worms are regarded as table delicacies.
* You can wash your sash with the blue: an allusion to an ancient poem—O the blue waves are limpid, / Wherewith I can wash my sash. It's an indication of detachedness and purity.

自广平乘醉走马六十里至邯郸登城楼览古书怀

醉骑白花骆，
西走邯郸城。
扬鞭动柳色，
写鞯春风生。
入郭登高楼，
山川与云平。
深宫翳绿草，
万事伤人情。
相如章华巅，
猛气折秦嬴。
两虎不可斗，
廉公终负荆。
提携裤中儿，
杵臼及程婴。
空孤就白刃，
必死耀丹诚。
平原三千客，
谈笑尽豪英。
毛君能颖脱，
二国且同盟。
皆为黄泉土，
使我涕纵横。
磊磊石子冈，
萧萧白杨声。
诸贤没此地，
碑版有残铭。

太古共今时，
由来互哀荣。
伤哉何足道，
感激仰空名。
赵俗爱长剑，
文儒少逢迎。
闲从博陵游，
帐饮雪朝酲。
歌酣易水动，
鼓震丛台倾。
日落把烛归，
凌晨向燕京。
方陈五饵策，
一使胡尘清。

An Impromptu on the Wall Tower of Hantan After Travelling Twenty Miles from Broadpeace While Drunk Astride My Horse

So drunk, a piebald horse I ride
To the town Hantan in the west.
I whip and stir the willow hue
While the bits are by wind caressed.
Now in the town I climb a tower
And see the hills with the clouds flow.
The deep palace is rank with grass;
Everything here stirs up one's woe.
There on the top of Flora Mound,
Lin crushed Ch'in's Lord with his brave air.
As two tigers should not contend,

Lien, to yield, did at last thorns bear.
The babe was hidden in the gown,
Saved by two martyrs, as all know.
So loyal, Ch'engying braved the blade;
His sacrifice like stars did glow.
Prince Plain's three thousand hangers-on,
Talking, laughing, were all great men.
Mao was like an awl shining out;
Two nations became allies then.
Now all these heroes have turned dust,
Which makes me shed tears with a bow.
They were noble just like Stone Mound,
Where poplar trees waved with a sough.
These saints lie buried underground;
The worn tablets show what they've cast.
Real worthies have posthumous fame,
As is true now just like the past.
What's the use of sadness and rue?
Fame is what one may try in vain.
Chao loved playing of his long sword,
So greet him all scholars would fain.
For leisure he toured with his friends,
Eating snow and sleeping so sound.
Their song could quake the River Change;
Their drum would topple Cluster Mound.
At dusk, with candles they returned
In the morn they left for Yan Town.
His friends offered him Five-bait Plan
So that Hun dust would be pressed down.

* Hantan: the former capital of the State of Chao in the Eastern Chough dynasty,

located in present-day Hopei Province.
* Broadpeace: referring to Kuangp'ing if transliterated, a county in present-day Hantan, Hopei Province.
* Flora Mound: built in the Spring and Autumn period.
* Lin: referring to Hsiangju Lin, a renowned statesman and diplomat of Chao. Ch'in and Chao had an agreement on exchanging fifteen towns with Ho's Jade. King Glare of Ch'in met Lin on Flora Mound to accept Ho's Jade. As Ch'in would not give the fifteen towns, Lin pretended to break the jade and successfully threatened the king.
* Ch'in's Lord: King Glare of Ch'in (reigning 306 B.C.– 251 B.C.), who weakened other six powers and laid the foundation for Ch'in's unification of China.
* tiger: a large carnivorous feline mammal of Asia, with vertical black wavy stripes on a tawny body and black bars or rings on the limbs and tail, praised as king of all animals.
* Lien: referring to P'o Lien, a renowned commander of Chao. Lien was a meritorious general but he envied Hsiangju Lin for he thought Lin was only good at gabbing. Lin remained polite in spite of Lien's disrespect because he had to put personal dispute aside to keep their state secured. Knowing that, Lien felt ashamed and carried thorns on his back to ask for forgiveness.
* two martyrs: referring to Ch'uchiu Lordson (? – 597 B.C.) and Ying Ch'eng (? – 583 B.C.), righteous men from Chin. When their lord was slaughtered, they sacrificed Lordson's life and Ch'eng's baby to save the lord's baby.
* Prince Plain: referring Lord Plain of Chao (? – 253 B.C.), one of the Four Childes in the Warring States period.
* Mao: referring to Sui Mao (285 B.C. – 228 B.C.), a lobbyist from Chao who recommended himself to visit Ch'u and gained his fame by making an alliance between Ch'u and Chao.
* Stone Mound: actually a mountain, where was the mausoleum of Yang Chao (? – 458 B.C.), the founder of the State of Chao.
* poplar: any of a genus (*Populus*) of dioecious trees and bushes of the willow family, widely distributed in the northern hemisphere.
* Chao: referring to Lord Plain of Chao, one of the Four Childes in the Warring States period.
* the River Change: the river by which Chingk'e bade farewell to his lord and friend, and set off for his mission.
* Cluster Mound: a mound northeast of Hantan.
* Yan Town: the capital of the State of Yan, today's Peking.
* Five-baits Plan: the plan to destroy a state with five baits—clothing and carts to mar

the eye, dainties and delicacies to mar the taste, music and women to mar the ear, houses, barns and maids to mar the abdomen; lord's grace and feats and entertainments to mar the mind.

月夜金陵怀古

苍苍金陵月，
空悬帝王州。
天文列宿在，
霸业大江流。
绿水绝驰道，
青松摧古丘。
台倾鸡鹊观，
宫没凤凰楼。
别殿悲清暑，
芳园罢乐游。
一闻歌玉树，
萧瑟后庭秋。

My Moonlit Recall of the Past in Gold Hill

Pale, pale, the moon over Gold Hill
To the Lords' Empire in vain glows.
The constellation shines above;
Their power's gone as the River flows.
Green pines stand upon the tombs old,
No more green along the Broad Way;
Courts and Phoenix Tower are all gone;
Jay Mound has fallen to decay.
So dreary looks Cool Summer Hall,
No more pleasure in the park now.
Jade Trees, the song heard here before,

> Has turned into a backyard sough.

* Gold Hill: referring to Nanking, one of the most well-known ancient capitals in China.
* the Lords' Empire: Gold Hill (today's Nanking) was chosen as capital by six kingdoms or empires before the T'ang dynasty.
* the River: the Yangtze River, i.e., the lower part of the Long River, the longest river in China.
* the Broad Way: referring to the mausoleums in Gold Hill.
* Courts and Phoenix Tower: ancient palaces.
* Jay Mound: an ancient palace.
* Cool Summer Hall: former palace built in the Chin dynasty.
* *Jade Trees*: the last emperor of Ch'en wrote a verse and ordered women in the palace to learn and sing it, which reads: The jade trees in the back court bloom/ For a while before dying in gloom.

金 陵 新 亭

金陵风景好，
豪士集新亭，
举目山河异，
偏伤周顗情。
四坐楚囚悲，
不忧社稷倾。
王公何慷慨，
千载仰雄名。

Kiosk New in Gold Hill

Gold Hill puts on a scenic view;
Peers and gents gather in Kiosk New.
Seen afar, it's a different land,
Whose scars, Marquis Chou can't stand.
Like prisoners, they lament their fate;
Who'll deplore the fall of the state?
O how far-visioned Lord Wang's aim!
For ages we've sung of his name.

* Kiosk New: a buttress built in the Six Dynasties period, an important military stronghold south of Gold Hill (called Health then), a doorway of the imperial palace.
* Gold Hill: referring to Nanking, one of the most well-known ancient capitals in China.
* Marquis Chou: referring to Ee Chou (A.D. 269 – A.D. 322), a commander of high reputation in the Chin dynasty. He once lamented for the perish of Western Chin.
* Lord Wang: referring to Tao Wang (A.D. 276 – A.D. 339), a statesman, calligrapher, and one of the founding lords of Eastern Chin.

庭 前 晚 开 花

西王母桃种我家，
三千阳春始一花。
结实苦迟为人笑，
攀折唧唧长咨嗟。

It Blooms Late in My Yard

In my yard grows a Mother West peach tree,
Which blooms once only in three thousand years.
It fruits too late, all people jeer at me;
I sway a branch and sigh long: jeers on jeers.

* Mother West peach tree: the peach tree planted by Mother West, which blooms once in three thousand years and bears fruits once in three thousand years.

宣州长史弟昭赠余琴谿中双舞鹤诗以见志

令弟佐宣城，
赠余琴谿鹤。
谓言天涯雪，
忽向窗前落。
白玉为毛衣，
黄金不肯博。
背风振六翮，
对舞临山阁。
顾我如有情，
长鸣似相托。
何当驾此物，
与尔腾寥廓。

Secretary of Hsuan's Brother Gives Me a Pair of Cranes Called Lute Stream, So I Compose This Poem to Express My Gratitude

Your bro helps you in Hsuan, and he
Gives two cranes called Lute Stream to me.
As said, they seem like skyline snow
That with wind to my sill does blow.
How white their plumage is, behold!
One will not exchange them for gold.
They flutter through the wind to trill
And dance before the tower uphill.
They look back to me with love deep;

For love one can trust their long cheep.
O when can we these creatures ride
To tour the blue sky side by side?

* crane: one of a family of large, long-necked, long-legged, heronlike birds allied to the rails, a symbol of integrity and longevity in Chinese culture, only second to the phoenix in cultural importance.
* Hsuan: an ancient town in present-day Hsuan, Anhui Province, a county instituted early in the Ch'in dynasty, and a prefecture instituted in the Chin dynasty. It is well known for rich historical legacies, and best remembered for its high-quality rice paper.

暖 酒

热暖将来镔铁文，
暂时不动聚白云。
拨却白云见青天，
掇头里许便成仙。

Warming Wine

I warm wine, the ripples like pattern steel;
Not stirred, like white clouds its face does appeal.
The white clouds swept off, the sky I can see;
If inside, an immortal one could be.

* pattern steel: a kind of alloyed steel introduced from Persia in the Southern and Northern Dynasties period, the material for the making of weapons like the long-handled hammers, long swords and so on.

戏 赠 杜 甫

饭颗山头逢杜甫,
顶戴笠子日卓午。
借问别来太瘦生,
总为从前作诗苦。

A Poem to Fu Tu for Fun

At Mt. Meal Grain I come across Fu Tu,
Who at noon wears a hat made of bamboo.
Why have you grown thin since I saw you last?
Verse composition's hard now like the past.

* Fu Tu: Fu Tu (A.D. 712 - A.D. 770), a realistic poet in the T'ang dynasty, one of the greatest poets in the history, regarded as "Saint of Poetry" in contrast with Pai Li, "God of Poetry", and Wei Wang, "Buddha of Poetry". Fu Tu was a grandson of Shenyan Tu (cir. A.D. 645 - cir. A.D. 708), another famous poet and high-ranking official.
* Mt. Meal Grain: a mountain located near Long Peace, as has been said.

寒　女　吟

昔君布衣时，
与妾同辛苦。
一拜五官郎，
便索邯郸女。
妾欲辞君去，
君心便相许。
妾读蘼芜书，
悲歌泪如雨。
忆昔嫁君时，
曾无一夜乐。
不是妾无堪，
君家妇难作。
起来强歌舞，
纵好君嫌恶。
下堂辞君去，
去后悔遮莫。

A Sad Wife's Croon

When you lived a poor and plain life,
I shared with you all pains in strife.
The day married to you I got,
A maiden from Hantan you sought.
Then I would from you go away;
You promised you would with me stay.
When I was looking at *Sweet Grass*,

My tears dropped like a rain, alas.
Ever since our wedding that year,
Not one night have I had good cheer.
It's not me that is hard to please,
A wife of yours can't be at ease.
If to dance I manage to rise,
You will turn and do me despise.
Now from you I will go away;
Regret? Regret in depth you may.

* Hantan: a city more than 3,100 years old, the capital of the State of Chao (403 B.C.- 222 B.C.) in the Eastern Chough dynasty (770 B.C.- 256 B.C.), located in present-day Hopei Province. This city was built in the Shang dynasty (cir. 1600 B.C.- cir. 1046 B.C.) and an imperial palace was built here for King Chow (cir. 1105 B.C.- 1046 B.C.) according to *Lonely Bamboo Annals*. The legacies and ruins bespeak the splendor of its glorious past.

会　别　离

结发生别离，
相思复相保。
如何日已久，
五变庭中草。
渺渺大海途，
悠悠汉江岛。
但恐不出门，
出门无远道。
远道行既难，
家贫衣复单。
严风吹积雪，
晨起鼻何酸。
人生各有志，
岂不怀所安。
分明天上日，
生死愿同欢。

Hope for a Reunion

We stayed and then we were apart;
Craving, I would cling to your heart.
For long, my life has been so hard;
Grass has dried five times in the yard.
The sea expands many a mile;
From far there appears the Han Isle.
As said, it never rains but pours;

If outdoors, you're far off outdoors.
Far off outdoors, it's a hard tour;
Thin clothes you wear, as we are poor.
The wind to the heavy snow blows;
Now up, sour I feel on my nose.
As everyone has his own will,
Why don't we repose and keep still?
So clear and so bright is the sun;
I would join you, combined as one.

* Grass has dried five times in the yard: an indirect speech of saying five years.
* the Han Isle: unidentified.

初　月

玉蟾离海上，
白露湿花时。
云畔风生爪，
沙头水浸眉。
乐哉弦管客，
愁杀战征儿。
因绝西园赏，
临风一咏诗。

The Crescent

The jade toad does rise from the sea,
When wet with dew the blossoms be.
The clouded wind does sway its claws;
The submerged shoal does raise its brows.
The musicians play well, how glad!
The front fighters fight hard, how sad!
From Western Garden kept away,
Before the wind I sing my lay.

* jade toad: the moon. What is "moon" in Chinese is an important image in Chinese literature or culture, with at least two hundred names, like Jade Mound (yaot'ai), Fair Lady (ts'anchüan), Jade Hare (yüt'u), White Hare (pait'u), Siver Hare (yint'u), Ice Hare (pingt'u), Gold Hare (chint'u), Hare Gleam (t'uhui), and so on.
* Western Garden: an allusion to Chih Ts'ao's poem, of which the first four lines are: His Highness does love to play host; / The feast over, he's still with zest. / At night, in the Western Garden, / They drive around, crest after crest.

雨 后 望 月

四郊阴霭散，
开户半蟾生。
万里舒霜合，
一条江练横。
出时山眼白，
高后海心明。
为惜如团扇，
长吟到五更。

Looking at the Moon After a Rain

When mist disappears, seen no more,
I see half the toad out the door.
Ten thousand miles see frost so bright;
The river spreads out like cloth white.
When it's rising, the hills look clear;
When it's risen, the sea seems near.
Just because I love this round moon,
Till daybreak I stay up and croon.

* the toad: the jade toad or the moon, an important image in Chinese Literature. In traditional times, a vagrant usually sat quietly on a moonlit night, particularly under a full moon, thinking of someone far away, inside the vast reaches of China proper and even overseas, who might himself or herself be sitting sharing the same moon at the same time, in the same reverent silence.

对　　雨

卷帘聊举目，
露湿草绵芊。
古岫披云氅，
空庭织碎烟。
水纹愁不起，
风线重难牵。
尽日扶犁叟，
往来江树前。

Facing the Rain

I look outside, drawing the screen;
Dew shines on the grass soft and green.
The olden cave hides clouds within;
The vacant yard's filled with mist thin.
The waves push my woe up and down;
The string's too thin to raise my frown.
The farmer's busy with his plough;
The riverside trees send him a sough.

* screen: a curtain which separates or cuts off, shelters or protects as a light partition, a common image in Chinese literature. Two lines from a Sung lyric by Haowen Yüan reads like this: "The drizzle falls before my tower's sill; / 'Broidered with crabapples, the screen's chill."

晓　　晴

野凉疏雨歇，
春色遍萋萋。
鱼跃青池满，
莺吟绿树低。
野花妆面湿，
山草纽斜齐。
零落残云片，
风吹挂竹溪。

Clearing Up at Dawn

The rain brings the field a chill hush;
The spring hue greens the grass so lush.
In the brimming pool some fish leap;
To the green trees orioles cheep.
The wild flowers put on a wet face;
The hill grass spreads like a curved lace.
Sparse clouds seem to float to and fro;
The bamboo creek feels a wind blow.

* oriole: golden oriole, one of the family of passerine birds, which looks bright yellow with contrasting black wings and sings beautiful songs.

望 夫 石

仿佛古容仪，
含愁带曙辉。
露如今日泪，
苔似昔年衣。
有恨同湘女，
无言类楚妃。
寂然芳霭内，
犹若待夫归。

The O-Come-Hubby Stone

It's an old look, so old it seems;
With sadness it sees dawning beams.
The dewdrops look like today's tears;
The moss is a veil from past years.
It's grieving like Hsiang Ladies' rue,
And speechless like Lady Ch'u's woe.
Silent, it's enshrouded in haze;
Is its man coming to its gaze?

* the O-Come-Hubby Stone: located in today's Shantung Province. A husband of Ch'i was summoned to hard work only three days after his wedding. Years after years, the wife climbed high to wait for her husband and finally turned to a rock standing firmly on top of the mountain.
* Hsiang Ladies: referring to Fairgrand and Shebloom, i.e., Lord Mound's two daughters married to Hibiscus. When Hibiscus was away on a south expedition, the two ladies went to look for him. When they heard their husband had died at Mt. Blue and

had been buried at Mt. Nine Doubts, they cried, each embracing a bamboo until they breathed their last, having shed all their tears.

* Lady Ch'u: formerly Marquise of Hsi during the Spring and Autumn period. In 680 B.C., King Civil of Ch'u conquered Hsi and took the marquise as his wife. Though Lady Hsi bore him two children, she had never spoken to him ever since she was taken. When asked why, she replied: "A wife serving two husbands, what do I have to say while unable to die?"

冬日归旧山

未洗染尘缨，
归来芳草平。
一条藤径绿，
万点雪峰晴。
地冷叶先尽，
谷寒云不行。
嫩篁侵舍密，
古树倒江横。
白犬离村吠，
苍苔壁上生。
穿厨孤雉过，
临屋旧猿鸣。
木落禽巢在，
篱疏兽路成。
拂床苍鼠走，
倒箧素鱼惊。
洗砚修良策，
敲松拟素贞。
此时重一去，
去合到三清。

Returning to the Old Hills on a Winter Day

My cap is not washed, washed it's not;
I'm back to the level grass lot.
The path is covered with canes green;

Countless peaks are veiled with snow clean.
No leaves left on the frozen ground;
Clouds stagnant o'er the dale ice bound.
The bamboo grove is dense with shacks;
The old trees pile upstream like stacks.
Some white dogs from the village bark;
Green moss on the wall now turns dark.
O'er the kitchen a pheasant flies;
Near the cottage a monkey cries.
When leaves fall down, nests do not fail;
If traps are sparse, beasts make a trail.
The bed shaken, rats escape out;
My cask emptied, bugs jump about.
The inkslab washed, I'll make advise;
Grinding the ink, I'll write verse nice.
Now I'll be marching on my way;
Go fulfill my great aim I may.

* Old Hills: probably referring to the Tait'ien Mountains.
* dog: a domesticated carnivorous mammal (*Canis familiaris*), of worldwide distribution and many varieties, noted for its adaptability and its devotion to man. The dog was domesticated in China at least 8,000 years ago and used as a hunter, as a poem in *The Book of Songs* says: "The dog bells clink and clink; / The hunter's handsome, a real pink."
* moss: a tiny, delicate green bryophytic plant growing on damp decaying wood, wet ground, humid rocks or trees, producing capsules which open by an operculum and contain spores. Under a poet's writing brush, it may arouse a poetic feeling or imagination.
* pheasant: a long-tailed gallinaceous bird noted for the gorgeous plumage of the male.
* monkey: any of a group of primates having elongate limbs, hands and feet adapted for grasping, and a highly developed nervous system, including marmosets, baboons, and macaques, but not the anthropoid apes, though monkeys and apes are used alternatively in Chinese.

* inkslab: a utensil where an ink stick is ground with water to dissolve before writing begins. It is one of the four treasures in a Chinese study, the other three stationeries being ink, paper and writing brush.

邹衍谷

燕谷无暖气,
穷岩闭严阴。
邹子一吹律,
能回天地心。

Yan Tsou's Dale

The northern dale's not warm, so cold;
Rocks, crags and shades do it enfold.
When Tsou a melody did play,
Heaven and earth ran their right way.

* Yan Tsou: Yan Tsou (324 B.C.- 250 B.C.), a representative scholar of Wordism and the founder of Five Elements Theory. Tsou suffered from false imprisonment by King Boon of Yan, who believed in slander against Tsou. The false imprisonment caused a blast of hoarfrost in June.
* Yan Tsou's Dale: also known as Millet Dale. When Yan Tsou lived in the dale, often playing a melody, the cold dale became warm and millet grew there, hence the name Yan Tsou's Dale or Millet Dale.

入清溪行山中

轻舟去何疾!
已到云林境。
起坐鱼鸟间,
动摇山水影。
岩中响自合,
溪里言弥静。
无事令人幽,
停桡向余景。

Boating on a Brook in the Mountains

How fast the skiff does run, swish, swish.
Now it has reached a clouded glade.
We rise and sit with birds and fish,
Swaying the hills that cast their shade.
One may hear rocks give off a sound;
Speaking makes the brook more serene.
Nothingness can make one profound;
I stop my oar to view the scene.

* skiff: a light rowboat for fishing or lotus-picking and so on; formerly a sailing vessel.
* glade: a clearing or open space in a luxuriant wood. Natural places like coves, glades, hills, moors, rivers, mounts and seas, and so on often allude to reclusion in Chinese culture.
* nothingness: a state of non-existence. Both Wordism and Christianity propagate the doctrine of the very beginning of the universe as nothing, out of which all were generated, that is, *ex nihilo*. Nothingness is also practiced in meditation, and even in governance in Wordism.

日出东南隅行

秦楼出佳丽,
正值朝日光。
陌头能驻马,
花处复添香。

The Sun Rises in the Southeast

Out of Ch'in Tower looks a dear one,
Who does bask in the morning sun.
Now one stops his horse on the lane,
While from the blooms balm wafts again.

* The Sun Rises in the Southeast: an allusion to a Han Conservatoire poem, the first lines read like this: Out of southeast rises the sun/ That Ch'in Mansion does lustre don. / The Ch'ins have a girl in good style, / Who calls herself Lofu to smile.
* Ch'in Tower: the building of the Ch'in family.
* horse: a large herbivorous solid-hoofed quadruped (*Equus caballus*) with a coarse mane and tail, of various strains: Ferghana, Mongolian, Kazaks, Hequ, Karasahr and so on, and of various colors: black, white, yellow, brown, dappled and so on, commonly in the domesticated state, employed as a beast of draught and burden and especially for riding upon.

代佳人寄翁参枢先辈

等闲经夏复经寒，
梦里惊嗟岂暂安。
南家风光当世少，
西陵演浪过江难。
周旋小字桃灯读，
重叠遥山隔雾看。
真是为君餐不得，
书来莫说更加餐。

To Respected Ts'anshu Weng in My Wife's Words

All summer and winter idled away,
Frights and sighs in my dream, I can't still stay.
In Southern Land few sights or scenes there are;
In Westridge, the tides and waves people bar.
The words are too small to read neath the lamp;
The hills far away loom veiled with mist damp.
In your absence, I'm in no mood for food;
Your news arrived! For food I'm in no mood!

* Southern Land: the land south of the Long River.
* Westridge: one of the three gorges of the Long River, the other two being Big Pond Gorge and Witch Gorge.

送 客 归 吴

江村秋雨歇，
酒尽一帆飞。
路历波涛去，
家惟坐卧归。
岛花开灼灼，
汀柳细依依。
别后无馀事，
还应扫钓矶。

Seeing Off My Guest to Wu

River village sees the rain stop;
After our toast, his sail does fly.
He's gone on waves that rise or drop;
Back at home I sit or else lie.
The flowers burst ablaze on the isle;
The willow waves adieu alone.
After parting, I've some free while,
So I should sweep the fishing stone.

* The flowers burst ablaze: an allusion to a poem in *Airs of the States* from *The Book of Songs*: The peach twigs sway, / Ablaze the flower.
* The willow waves adieu: an allusion to a poem in *Psalms Minor* from *The Book of Songs*: When we left long ago, / The willows waved adieu.

送友生游峡中

风静杨柳垂，
看花又别离。
几年同在此，
今日各驱驰。
峡里闻猿叫，
山头见月时。
殷勤一杯酒，
珍重岁寒姿。

Seeing Off My Friend to Tour the Gorge

No wind, the willows droop their twigs;
The flowers seen, you're going away.
We've been together a few years;
And will run different ways today.
In the gorge you'll hear monkeys cry
And see the moon atop the hill.
Please take one more cup to cheer up;
Take care of yourself in days chill.

* willow: any of a large genus of shrubs and trees related to poplars, having generally smooth branches, and often long, slender, pliant, and sometimes pendent branchlets, a symbol of farewell or nostalgia in Chinese culture. The best image is in *Vetch We Pick*, a verse in *The Book of Songs*, which is like this: When we left long ago, / The willows waved adieu. / Now back to our home town, / We meet snow falling down.
* monkey: any of a group of primates usually having a flat, hairless face, elongate limbs, hands and feet adapted for grasping, and a highly developed nervous system,

including marmosets, baboons, and macaques, but not the anthropoid apes, though monkeys and apes are used alternatively in Chinese, also used as a metaphor for somebody who is mischevious and shrewdly calculating.

送袁明府任长沙

别离杨柳青，
樽酒表丹诚。
古道携琴去，
深山见峡迎。
暖风花绕树，
秋雨草沿城。
自此长江内，
无因夜犬惊。

Seeing Off Magistrate Yüan to Govern Long Sand

Now from the willow you will part;
Cup raised, I will express my heart.
With your lute, you'll go on the trail,
In the hills there met by a dale.
Wind warm, blossoms deck the trees tall;
Rain cold, grass sprawls along the wall.
You'll rule the Long River all right,
So no dogs need to bark at night.

* Long Sand: Ch'angsha if transliterated, a vassal state in the Han dynasty and now the capital city of present-day Hunan Province.
* the Long River: the longest river in China, originating from the T'angkula Mountains on Tibet Plateau, flowing through 11 provincial areas, more than 6,300 kilometers long, the third longest river in the world.
* dog: a domesticated carnivorous mammal (Canis familiaris), of worldwide distribution

and many varities, noted for its adaptability and its devotion to man. The dog was domesticated in China at least 8,000 years ago and was often used as a hunter, as a poem in *The Book of Songs* says: "The dog bells clink and clink; / The hunter's handsome, a real pink."

送史司马赴崔相公幕

峥嵘丞相府,
清切凤凰池。
羡尔瑶台鹤,
高栖琼树枝。
归飞晴日好,
吟弄惠风吹。
正有乘轩乐,
初当学舞时。
珍禽在罗网,
微命若游丝。
愿托周南羽,
相衔溪水湄。

Seeing Off Commander Shih to Serve Under Premier Ts'ui

Premier's Hall has a splendid look;
Phoenix Pool's as clear as can be.
All admire the crane neath the moon,
Which will perch on a nectar tree.
It flies towards the shining sun
And chants to the wind with romance.
Like riding in a sedan car,
Like learning a roundelay dance.
The rare bird is trapped in a net,
Prone to die, struggling there, so weak.

May it fly up with its strong wings

To the creek with seed in its beak.

* Premier's Hall: a premier's office, which originated in the Three Kingdoms period.
* Phoenix Pool: a pool by Privy Council (Central Secretariat Department), near the emperor, hence the name; referring to a premier of Privy Council.
* crane: one of a family of large, long-necked, long-legged, heronlike birds allied to the rails, a symbol of integrity and longevity in Chinese culture, only second to the phoenix in cultural importance.
* nectar tree: a legendary tree that is twenty thousand meters tall and three hundred meters in circumference.

战　城　南

战地何昏昏，
战士如群蚁。
气重日轮红，
血染蓬蒿紫。
乌乌衔人肉，
食闷飞不起。
昨日城上人，
今日城下鬼。
旗色如罗星，
鼙声殊未已。
妾家夫与儿，
俱在鼙声里。

Fighting South of the Town

The soldiers are like swarms of ants;
So dusty is the battleground.
The sun in heavy haze looks red;
The crown daisies are in blood drowned.
The crows have man flesh in their beak;
Their food so heavy, they can't fly.
Those on the town wall yesterday
Today below the town wall lie.
Flags shine like the constellation;
Drums are beaten loud all around.
Poor, my husband, o poor my sons,

They are all there, in the drum sound.

* crown daisy: also known as crown daisy chrysanthemum, a green plant with a thin white stem, which can be used as a vegetable.
* crow: an omnivorous, raucous, oscine bird of the genus *Corvus*, with glossy black plumage. It is regarded as an ominous bird, a metaphor for death because it is a scavenger feeding on carrion. It is a common image in Chinese literature, which can be found in *The Book of Songs* compiled 2,500 years ago: "Crows are all black, it's said, / So as foxes are red."

胡 无 人 行

十万羽林儿，
临洮破郅支。
杀添胡地骨，
降足汉营旗。
塞阔牛羊散，
兵休帐幕移。
空馀陇头水，
呜咽向人悲。

Hun, There Will Be None

Ten thousand men of Armed Escort,
Lint'ao they take! Huns' chief they beat!
The Hun corpses all o'er the ground,
The soldiers beneath their flags meet.
Cattle and sheep dot the broad ranch;
Camps are removed now ends the war.
But a spring gurgles from Mt. Bulge,
Which does the tragedy deplore.

* Armed Escort: imperial guarding Corps, established by Emperor Martial in Western Han.
* Lint'ao: Lint'ao County under today's Settled West (Tinghsi), Kansu Province, one of the fountainheads of the Yellow River culture, instituted as a county in 384 B.C. though with a different name and changed to the present name in 1929. It is entitled as Town of Poetry, Town of Horticulture, Town of Flowers and so on.
* Mt. Bulge: a mountain located in the southeast of present-day Kansu Province, 2,928 meters above sea level and about 240 kilometers long from north to south, the borderline between Sha'anhsi Loess Plateau and West Bulge Loess Plateau.

鞠 歌 行

丽莫似汉宫妃，
谦莫似黄家女。
黄女持谦齿发高，
汉妃恃丽天庭去。
人生容德不自保，
圣人安用推天道。
君不见，蔡泽嵌枯诡怪之形状，
大言直取秦丞相。
又不见田千秋才智不出人，
一朝富贵如有神。
二侯行事在方册，
泣麟老人终困厄。
夜光抱恨良叹悲，
日月逝矣吾何之。

A Football Song

None is as lovely as Sis Wang Glare;
None is as modest as Sis Huang fair.
Modest, Huang had pearly teeth and hair tall;
Lovely, Wang was sent from Celestial Hall.
E'en with great worth, one can't himself protect;
All in vain, a saint does the Word respect.
Don't you espy, Tse Ts'ai, deformed, hither so fat, thither so thin,
Being glib, he became premier of Ch'in?
And don't you see Ever T'ien has no intelligence high,

With wealth and power, he is God-like, so spry?
These two peers were into records written;
Confucius, wise, was poverty-stricken.
So grieved, all night I only sigh and sigh;
What could I do now while time runs to fly?

* Sis Wang Glare: referring to Lady Glare, Chaochün Wang if transliterated, a lady in the seraglio of the emperor of the Han dynasty, one of the Four Belles in China. A maid of honour in the beginning, she was selected in 33 B.C. to marry the Hun chieftain who had proposed a royal marriage to consolidate mutual peace. She was one of the earliest victims of the political marriages, which the ruling house of China was compelled to make from time to time with the chieftains of the barbarian tribes in order to avoid their savage incursions into China, the Middle Kingdom.
* Sis Huang: Lord Huang of Ch'i had two daughters who were extremely beautiful and charming, but due to Lord Huang's modesty, the two girls were said to be ugly. When they were at the marriageable age, nobody came to make engagement with them.
* the Word: referring to Tao if transliterated, the most significant and profoundest concept in Chinese philosophy. According to Laocius's *The Word and the World*: "The Word is void, but its use is infinite. O deep! It seems to be the root of all things."
* Tse Ts'ai: a premier of Ch'in in the Warring States period.
* Ch'in: the Ch'in State or the State of Ch'in (905 B.C.- 206 B.C.), one of the most powerful vassal states in the Chough dynasty, which developed into the first unified regime of China, i.e., the Ch'in Empire.
* Ever T'ien: Ever T'ien (? -77 B.C.), a highborn premier in the Han dynasty.
* Confucius: Confucius (551 B.C.- 479 B.C.), a renowned thinker, educator and statesman in the Spring and Autumn period, born in the State of Lu, who was the founder of Confucianism and who had exerted profound influence on Chinese culture. He is one of the few leaders who based their philosophy on the virtues that are required for the day-to-day living. His philosophy centered on personal and governmental morality, correctness of social relationships, justice and sincerity.

题许宣平庵壁

我吟传舍咏,
来访真人居。
烟岭迷高迹,
云林隔太虚。
窥庭但萧瑟,
倚杖空踌躇。
应化辽天鹤,
归当千岁馀。

An Inscription for the Wall of Hsu's Temple

While chanting *I'm Coming*, an ode,
I come to visit True Man's abode.
I feel lost while uphill I climb;
The woody forest's void of time.
As there I gaze, the yard is bleak;
With a vain stick, what can I seek?
May I be a crane in Liao's skies,
Which in a thousand years back flies!

* True Man: a Wordist term used to indicate those who have a thorough understanding of the nature of life and the cosmos.
* a crane in Liao's skies: As legend goes, Lingwei Ting, an immortal in East Liao in the Western Han dynasty, became a crane and flied back to his hometown, perched on a high stele, singing: Ting-ting, Ting-ting, an immortal crane, / In a thousand years I'm at home again.

题 峰 顶 寺

夜宿峰顶寺，
举手扪星辰。
不敢高声语，
恐惊天上人。

An Inscription for Temple on the Peak

Tonight at Temple-on-the-Peak,
I may pick up a star on high.
In a loud voice I dare not speak,
Lest I frighten those in the sky.

* Temple-on-the-Peak: the name of a peak about 50 kilometers from Yellow Plum (Huangmei) County, today's Hupei Province.

题舒州司空山瀑布

断崖如削瓜，
岚光破崖绿。
天河从中来，
白云涨川谷。
玉案赤文字，
世眼不可读。
摄身凌青霄，
松风拂我足。

An Inscription for Mt. Ssukung Waterfalls in Shuchow

Like a melon cut is the cliff;
The sunlight in mist breaks the cliff stiff.
From within, the Milky Way pours;
O'er the valley a white cloud soars.
The jade desk with red words inlaid,
Not for the world, but for gods made.
Rising, to the blue sky I look,
While a pine wind my feet does stroke.

* Mt. Ssukung: located in present-day Anch'ing, Anhui Province.
* Shuchow: an ancient city in today's Anhui Province.
* melon: a trailing plant of the gourd family, or its fruit. There are two genera, the muskmelon and the watermelon, each with numerous varieties, growing in both tropical and temperate zones.
* the Milky Way: the Silver River in Chinese mythology, a luminous band circling the heavens composed of stars and nebulae; the Galaxy.

断　句
Fragments

其　一

举袖露条脱，
招我饭胡麻。

No.1

Her raised sleeve sees her bracelet shine;
On my sesame meal you may dine.

* sesame: an East Indian herb, containing seeds which are used as food and as a source of the pale yellow sesame oil, used as salad oil or an emollient, introduced from Ferghana by Ch'ien Chang (164 B.C.- 114 B.C.), a diplomat, traveler, explorer, and the initiator of the Silk Road.

其 二

野禽啼杜宇，
山蝶舞庄周。

No. 2

The wild fowl to the cuckoo cries;
The butterfly with Sir Lush flies.

* fowl: the common domestic cock, hen or chicken, poultry in general. The domestication of the fowl in China was begun more than 5,000 years ago according to archaeological finds.
* cuckoo: the bird of homesickness in Chinese culture. It is said that during the Shang dynasty, Cuckoo (Yǔ Tu), a caring king of Shu, abdicated the throne due to a flood and lived in reclusion. After his death, he, the human Cuckoo, turned into a bird cuckoo, wailing day and night, shedding tears and blood.
* The butterfly with Sir Lush flies: Sir Lush (369 B.C.- 286 B.C.), a great thinker, philosopher and litterateur in the Warring States Period, wrote a fable about the indivisibility and metamorphosis of things, which reads like this—Once, Sir Lush dreamed that he transformed into a butterfly, a butterfly that flied so free, so carefree! It didn't know it was Lush. Suddenly, he woke up and, in a surprise, realized that he was Lush. Did Lush dream of being a butterfly or a butterfly of being Lush? There must be a demarcation between Lush and the butterfly. This is what is called metamorphosis.

阳 春 曲

芣苢生前径，
含桃落小园。
春心自摇荡，
百舌更多言。

A Tune of Sunny Spring

On the front pathway plantains sprawl;
In my small garden cherries fall.
My heart of spring swings, fall or rise,
While the mocking birds utter whys.

* plantain: an annual or perennial herb (genus *Plantago*) widely distributed in temperate regions, a kind of herbal medicine for infertility.
× mocking bird: a bird termed *Turdus merula* in Latin, noted for its rich song and the powers of imitating the calls of other birds.

舍 利 佛

金绳界宝地，
珍木荫瑶池。
云间妙音奏，
天际法螺吹。

Sariputra

Treasure Land's marked with a gold line;
Jade Pool's shaded by a tree fine.
Amid clouds rings a tune so fair;
A conch toots from the skyline there.

* Sariputra: one of the ten students of Buddha, known for wisdom.
* Treasure Land: In Buddhism, there is a country called Treasure Land because its borders are festooned with golden strings or ropes.
* Jade Pool: a fairy pool on Mt. Queen, by which Mother West used to hold banquets.
* conch: the large, spiral, univalve shell of any of various marine mollusks, often used as a trumpet.

摩多楼子

从戎向边北，
远行辞密亲。
借问阴山侯，
还知塞上人。

Mordor Tower

I take leave of my dear ones now,
As to North Land I start to go.
To Marquis of Mt. Shade I bow:
Any border man do you know?

* Mordor Tower: an ancient topic of Han conservatoire of music, usually about hunting or warfare.
* North Land: mainly the area north of the Huai River, one of the longest and most important rivers in China.
* Marquis of Mt. Shade: a gazer on Mt. Shade, which is on the northern border of China.

春　感

茫茫南与北，
道直事难谐。
榆荚钱生树，
杨花玉糁街。
尘紫游子面，
蝶弄美人钗。
却忆青山上，
云门掩竹斋。

Feeling the Spring

Lo, south, lo, north, all run between;
It's hard to keep the golden mean.
Pods look like coins on the elm tree;
Catkins fly downtown like grits wee.
Dust rises to the vagrant's face;
Butterflies play with the belle's lace.
On the green hills as I recall,
Thin clouds float to the bamboo stall.

* the golden mean: a well-balanced ideal state of things, as was proposed by Aristotle (384 B.C.- 322 B.C.), which is the same thing as moderation or equilibrium clarified in the doctrine of the mean promulgated by Confucius (551 B.C.- 479 B.C.). The philosophic connotations of the doctrine of the golden mean can be summarized as four principles, namely moderation, integrity, flexibility and harmony.
* elm: a deciduous shade tree of America, Europe and Asia (genus *Ulmus*), with a broad, spreading, or overarching top, whose sweet pods look like coins and are

delicious.
* catkin: a deciduous scaly spike of flowers, as in the willow, an image of helpless drifting or wandering in Chinese literature.
* bamboo stall: a simple shelter made of bamboo.

殷十一赠栗冈砚

殷侯三玄士，
赠我栗冈砚。
洒染中山毫，
光映吴门练。
天寒水不冻，
日用心不倦。
携此临墨池，
还如对君面。

Yin Eleven Gives Me a Chestnut Mound Slab

Marquis Yin called Scholar Profound
Gives me an ink slab, Chestnut Mound.
My Mid-hill writing brush is great,
Whose shine I splash to the Wu gate.
Though it's cold, the ink does not freeze;
Day by day, it does my heart please.
When with it by Ink Pool I rise,
I seem to be meeting your eyes.

* Chestnut Mound: the name of an inkslab only mentioned in this poem. Probably, this kind of inkslab was made of materials from Chestnut Mound.
* Marquis Yin: referring to Pai Li's friend that Pai Li was writing to, but who he was remains unidentified.
* ink slab: a utensil for the preparation of ink by grinding an ink stick with water on it.
* writing brush: any of various writing brushes or called Chinese brush, widely used for

writing or painting, invented or renovated by Tien Meng (259 B.C.- 210 B.C.), a general in the Ch'in dynasty.
* Ink Pool: the pool where the greatest calligrapher Hsichih Wang washed his writing brush, in Summit County, i.e., today's Shaohsing, Chechiang Province.

普 照 寺

天台国清寺，
天下为四绝。
今到普照游，
到来复何别。
柟木白云飞，
高僧顶残雪。
门外一条溪，
几回流岁月。

All Glare Temple

State Peace Temple called Altar Blessed
Is ranked one of the world's Four Best.
I've come to tour All Glare today;
Does this fane have its different way?
The phoebe zhennans to clouds grow;
The monks have on top thawing snow.
There flows a stream out of the door,
Which turns with time now as before.

* State Peace Temple: also known as Altar Blessed, a Buddhist temple located in today's Chechiang Province.
* the world's Four Best: the four most famous incomparable Buddhist temples in China, that is, Soul Crag Temple in Chichow, Jade Spring Temple in Chaste (Chingchow), Perching Cloud Temple in Junchow and State Peace Temple in Taichow.
* All Glare: All Glare Temple, the alias of State Peace Temple.
* phoebe zhennan: a tree of the genus *Machilus*, which can grow as tall as 30 meters, having hard precious wood, usually used in ship making and palace building.

钓　　台

磨尽石岭墨，
浔阳钓赤鱼。
霭峰尖似笔，
堪画不堪书。

Fishing Platform

I grind and grind the Inkridge ink,
And in Searchshine fish for fish pink.
Mt. Haze has a writing-brush look;
It makes a painting, not a book.

* Fishing Platform: 9 kilometers from today's Black (Ee if transliterated) County, Anhui Province, also known as Searchshine Platform.
* the Inkridge: Mt. Inkridge, 9 kilometers from Black County, from which black clay can be used as ink.
* Searchshine: Fishing Platform.
* Mt. Haze: 7.5 kilometers from Black County, steep like a writing brush.
* writing-brush: any of various writing brushes or called Chinese brush, widely used for writing or painting, invented or renovated by Tien Meng (259 B.C.- 210 B.C.), a general in the Ch'in dynasty.

小 桃 源

黟县小桃源,
烟霞百里间。
地多灵草木,
人尚古衣冠。
市向晡前散,
山经夜后寒。

A Small Fairyland

Scenic Black County all beguiles,
Where mist spreads out a hundred miles.
All magic herbs this place does boast;
Ancient clothes are adored the most.
The market's closed in the afternoon;
At dusk the hills turn cold so soon.

* Fairyland: a metaphor used for the beautiful place of Black County in today's Anhui Province.
* Black County: referring to Ee County in today's Anhui Province, so named because of Mt. Black nearby, instituted in 221 B.C., when the Ch'in Empire was founded. It is noted for its natural beauty and cultural heritage, located between Mt. Yellow and Mt. White.
* magic herbs: precious medicinal herbs like Lucid Ganoderma, ginseng, tuber of multiflower knotweed and so on.

題窦圖山

樵夫与耕者，
出入画屏中。

An Inscription for Mt. T'uan Tou

Farmers and woodcutters are seen
To shuttle on the painted screen.

* Mt. T'uan Tou: located in present-day Ssuch'uan Province. It is said that T'uan Tou, an immortal, used to live here, hence the name according to *Autographies of Immortals* compiled by Hsiang Liu, the King of Huainan in the Han dynasty.
* farmers and woodcutters: also used as a metaphor for hermits in Chinese culture.
* screen: a curtain which separates or cuts off, shelters or protects as a light partition, a common image in Chinese literature. Two lines from a Sung lyric by Haowen Yüan reads like this:"The drizzle falls before my tower's sill; / 'Broidered with crabapples, the screen's chill."

赠江油尉

岚光深院里，
傍砌水泠泠。
野燕巢官舍。
溪云入古厅。
日斜孤吏过，
帘卷乱峰青。
五色神仙尉，
焚香读道经。

To the Sheriff of Riveroil

Mist light into the yard does fall;
By the steps, water gurgles cold.
Swallows make nests on the beam;
Stream clouds float into the hall old.
The sun setting, a clerk goes by;
The screen drawn, the peaks cluster calm.
The sheriff who's free like a god
Now reads the Word in incense balm.

* Riveroil: Pai Li's hometown, a county in what is Ssuch'uan Province today. It was instituted as a prefecture in A.D. 505 and changed into a county later, inhabited by more than a dozen nationalities such as Mongolians, Hmongs, Tibetans, Yis, Huis, Manchus and so on except Han Chinese.
* the Word: the foundational concept of Wordism, which was advanced and elaborated by Laocius, a great philosopher in the Spring and Autumn period. The Word is identifiable with the Word or Logos in the West, as there is an enormous amount of

common ground in the two cosmologies and the doctrines concerning the most fundamental matters such as "the Word is the One" and "God is the One", and the personalization of Being, the progenitor of finite spirits, which are subordinate kinds of Being or merely appearances of the Divine, the One.

* incense: an aromatic substance that exhales perfume during combustion, burnt before a Buddhist, Wordist or any religious or ancestral figure as an act of worship, usually offered with a prayer or vow.

清 平 乐

Pure Peace Tune

其 一

禁庭春昼，
莺羽披新绣。
百草巧求花下斗，
只赌珠玑满斗。
日晚却理残妆，
御前闲舞霓裳。
谁道腰肢窈窕，
折旋笑得君王。

No. 1

The palace, a spring day,
Oriole plumes shining, new and gay.
For all herbs beneath blossoms they compete,
Betting on jewels and gems replete.
Now at night she makes up for romance
And before the Lord whirls a plumage dance.
Her slender waist does the Lord beguile
Into delight, a laugh or a smile.

---

* Pure Peace Tune: a subgenre of lyrics. Pai Li's way of life often led him to inns and winehouses where courtesans entertained guests with a popular song form called lyric (tz'u). Each lyric had a different song form, and poets would write lyrics that fit the music, which meant using irregular line lengths. Pai Li was one of the first to adopt this kind of song form, which culminated in the Sung dynasty (A.D. 960 – A.D. 1279).

* oriole plumes: costumes in bright hue like that of oriole plumes.
* plumage dance: a kind of court dance in the T'ang dynasty, to the accompaniment of a tune called Rainbow Plumage, which was believed to have been composed by Emperor Deepsire of T'ang.

其 二

禁闱秋夜,
月探金窗罅。
玉帐鸳鸯喷兰麝,
时落银灯香灺。
女伴莫话孤眠,
六宫罗绮三千。
一笑皆生百媚,
宸衷教在谁边?

No. 2

The palace, a fall night,
Into the window pries moon light.
From the censer wafts orchid-musk balm;
Betimes ash from the candle falls calm.
Does she sleep with the Lord, just a pair?
In the harem are three thousand belles rare.
All charming blossoms from just one smile;
Who does His Majesty's heart beguile?

* orchid-musk: precious incense made from orchid and musk extract, usually used in harems or some rich families in ancient China.
* candle: a cylinder of tallow, wax, or other solid fat, containing a wick, to give light when burning, first seen in literature in the Eastern Han dynasty. The most famous lines about candles are from a poem by a T'ang poet named Shangyin Li, "Silkworms stop offering silk when they die; / Candles become ash as their tears run dry."
* harem: a forbidden palace for wives and concubines in Chinese history. A harem could be very large. In the harem in the age of Emperor Martial (156 B.C.- 87 B.C.) or Emperor Vital (74 B.C.- 33 B.C.), there were 3,000 concubines in a hierarchical

structure of fourteen ranks. And in the Chin dynasty, Emperor Martial of Chin (A.D. 236 – A.D. 290) had 10,000 beauties and Emperor Deepsire of T'ang (A.D. 685 – A.D. 762) had 40,000.

清 平 乐 令
Pure Peace Tune

其 一

烟深水阔，
音信无由达。
唯有碧天云外月，
偏照悬悬离别。
尽日感事伤怀，
愁眉似锁难开。
夜夜长留半被，
待君魂梦归来。

No. 1

Mist thick, the waves roll far;
No news, I don't know where you are.
Only the moon out of the clouds on high
Gleams over the trace of our good-bye.
All day long I feel sorry, cast down,
My worried look and my knitted frown.
I leave half my quilt for you each night,
Waiting for your soul that might alight.

* soul: the rational, emotional and volitional faculties existing in man. In Wordist theology, it is an active consciousness or will that can go freely out of the constraint of the human body.

其 二

鸳衾凤褥，
夜夜常孤宿。
更被银台红蜡烛，
学妾泪珠相续。
花貌些子时光，
抛人远泛潇湘。
欹枕悔听寒漏，
声声滴断愁肠。

No. 2

In quilt of brocade bright
I sleep alone from night to night.
On the silver stand shine the candles red;
Continuously, bead-like tears I shed.
Although I am now in budding prime,
I'm left alone as if in South Clime.
The hourglass annoys me without end;
Drip after drip, it does my heart rend.

* candle: a cylinder of tallow, wax, or other solid fat, containing a wick, to give light when burning, first seen in literature in the Eastern Han dynasty. The most famous lines about candles are from a poem by a T'ang poet named Shangyin Li, "Silkworms stop offering silk when they die; / Candles become ash as their tears run dry."
* South Clime: referring to the area covering Long Sand, which belonged to the State of Ch'u and was made a vassal state in the Han dynasty, and now largely Hunan Province.
* hourglass: a vessel used for measuring time by the running of water or sand from the upper into the lower compartment, also used as metaphor for the elapse of time.

其 三

画堂晨起，
来报雪花坠。
高卷帘栊看佳瑞，
皓色远迷庭砌。
盛气光引炉烟，
素草寒生玉佩。
应是天仙狂醉，
乱把白云揉碎。

No. 3

In the bedroom I rise;
To send me tidings the snow flies.
I draw up the curtain for a good sight;
The snow dazzles the steps with its white.
The stove smoke is drawn by brightness bold;
The simple grass does ice trinkets hold.
The fairies must be so drunk, so high;
They have crumbled white clouds in the sky!

* fairies: imaginary human-like immortal beings abiding the sky and frequently visiting the earth. Half of Pai Li's world is another world. He dreamed of fairies, caroused with fairies and toasted to fairies, and he traveled to Fairyland, Fairy Castle, Fairy Palace, Fairy Isles, and so on and he himself was addressed as Fallen Fairy by his friend Chihchang Ho.

桂 殿 秋

仙女下，董双成，
汉殿夜凉吹玉笙。
曲终却从仙官去，
万户千门惟月明。
河汉女，玉炼颜，
云軿往往在人间。
九霄有路去无迹，
袅袅香风生佩环。

Autumn in Laurel Hall

A fairy does light,
Who's called Double Right.
She plays her jade flute in the hall at night.
The tune o'er, she disappears, seen no more,
All households are moonlit, from door to door.
The Milky Way maid,
Her face shines like jade.
Has she often in this human world stayed?
She has gone up to the skies without trace,
But her trinkets clink to her balmy grace.

* Laurel Hall: referring to Moon Palace. In Chinese mythology, there is a laurel tree on the moon, more than 1,500 meters tall, and it would never fall even though Kang Wu, an exiled immortal, kept cutting it.
* Double Right: It is said that Double Right is the jade girl beside Queen Mother.

* the Milky Way maid: referring to a fairy, the granddaughter of Emperor of Heaven. As legend goes, she and the worldly cowherd fell in love and gave birth to a son and a daughter. Their love was disclosed to Emperor of Heaven, who sent Queen Mother to take the fairy back to Heaven. While Cowherd was trying to catch up in a boat the cow had made with its horn broken, Queen Mother rived the air with her hair pin, so there appeared the Silver River, i.e., the Milky Way to keep them apart, and the fairy and the cowherd became two stars called Vega and Altair.

连 理 枝
Twigs Entwined

其 一

雪盖宫楼闭，
罗幕昏金翠。
斗压阑干，
香心澹薄，
梅梢轻倚。
喷宝猊香烬、
麝烟浓，
馥红绡翠被。

No. 1

The palace closed, with snow it's cold;
In the gauze net, the quilt shines gold.
The Dipper is above;
Her heart is tired, no love.
On the twigs she relies;
To the incense ember she sighs.
Good smells the musk smoke;
Her balmy silk quilt she does stroke.

* the Dipper: the Big Dipper, a constellation composed of seven bright stars, which looks like a spoon in the sky. The Dipper has an important position in Chinese literature, likened to an emperor or a personage of noble character and high prestige, or likened to a beacon for the guidance of one's career or pursuit.
* incense: an aromatic substance that exhales perfume during combustion, burnt before a

Buddhist, Wordist or any religious or ancestral figure as an act of worship.
* musk: a soft, reddish-brown powdery secretion of a penetrating odor, obtained from the preputial follicles of the male musk deer, used by perfumers and in medicine.

其 二

浅画云垂帔，
点滴昭阳泪。
咫尺宸居，
君恩断绝，
似遥千里。
望水晶帘外、
竹枝寒，
守羊车未至。

No. 2

Lo, thin mist painted on her shawl,
Drip after drip, her sad tears fall.
His room's near, the next door;
His love's gone, left no more.
He's too far off, in haze;
Out of the window she does gaze.
Cold, cold, the bamboo,
His goat sedan's not come, o rue.

* bamboo: a tall, tree-like or shrubby grass in tropical and semi-tropical regions, a symbol of altitude and rectitude, integrity and longevity, one of the four most important images in Chinese literature, which are wintersweet, orchid, bamboo and chrysanthemum.
* goat sedan: a fabulously decorated sedan car driven by a goat, usually for an emperor. Emperor Martial of Western Chin often made a tour in the harem where ten thousand concubines lived and would stop to spend the night with a lady where the goat stopped.

杂 题
Miscellanies

其 一

乘兴踏月，
西入酒家。
不觉人物两忘，
身在世外。

No. 1

Treading moonlight, so blessed,
Ent'ring the pub from west.
Unwitting, all and myself I forgot,
On earth if I were not?

* pub: Our poet Pai Li spent much time in pubs and taverns as the "spirit of poetry incarnate" and God of Wine, and for this reason he was judged or misjudged as morally sordid for his involvement with "women and wine" by Anshih Wang in the Sung dynasty.

其 二

夜来月下卧醒，
花影零乱，
满人衿袖，
疑如濯魄于冰壶也。

No. 2

There the moon, awake I lie under,
The flower shade asunder,
All o'er my sleeve, a lot,
As if my soul were cleansed in the ice pot.

* the moon: an image of solitude or purity in Chinese culture. The moon is celebrated with mooncakes at a family gathering on Mid-autumn Day when the moon is at its full glory. What is "moon" in Chinese has at least two hundred names based on a viewer's imagination and association, like Shade Spirit (yinp'o), Jade Mound (yaot'ai), Fair Lady (cha'anchüan), Jade Hare (yüt'u), White Hare (pait'u), Silver Hare (yint'u), Ice Hare (pingt'u), Gold Hare (chint'u), Hare Gleam (t'uhui), Laurel Soul (Kuip'o) and so on.
* ice pot: also called jade pot, a pot crystally bright, usually alluding to the purity of the holder's heart, and sometimes referring to the pure world of immortality, where elixirs are concocted.

其 三

楼虚月白，
秋宇物化。
于斯凭阑，
身势飞动。
非把酒自忘，
此兴何极？

No. 3

The tower void, the moon white,
All sleep on this fall night.
On the rail I rely,
As if I were to fly.
I forget all, holding my cup,
How were I so raised up?

* the moon: the satellite of the earth, an important image in Chinese literature or culture as it can evoke many associations such as solitude and nostalgia on the one hand, and purity, brightness and happy reunions on the other. Philosophically, It is the very germ or source of *Shade*, and the sun is its *Shine* counterpart. What is "moon" in Chinese has at least two hundred names, like Shade Spirit (yinp'o), Jade Mound (yaot'ai), Fair Lady (cha'anchüan), Jade Hare (yüt'u), White Hare (pait'u), Silver Hare (yint'u), Ice Hare (pingt'u), Gold Hare (chint'u), Hare Gleam (t'uhui), Laurel Soul (Kuip'o) and so on.
* raised up: Pai Li used to end up drunk, a state or an ecstasy, in which he was released fully into his most authentic and enlightened self—quietism as spontaneity.

其　四

吾头懵懵，
试书此不能自辨，
贺生为我读之。

No. 4

I have a dizzy head;
The words so blurred, how can the book be read?
Mr. Ho reads it out to me instead.

* Mr. Ho: unidentified, probably Chihchang Ho (A.D. 659 - cir. A.D. 744), Pai Li's friend, a famous poet and calligrapher in the T'ang dynasty.

立 冬

冻笔新诗懒写，
寒炉美酒时温。
醉看墨花月白，
恍疑雪满前村。

Beginning of Winter

Writing brush frozen, not fain to write;
Cold stove, warming fire, mellow wine.
Drunk, I see the moonlit ink turn white;
The village looms full of snow to shine.

* Beginning of Winter: the beginning of the winter season falls on the 7th or 8th of November. As a term it is one of the 19th of the twenty-four solar terms, which are as follows: Beginning of Spring (1st solar term), Rain Water (2nd solar term), Waking of Insects (3rd solar term), Spring Equinox (4th solar term), Pure Brightness (5th solar term), Grain Rain (6th solar term), Beginning of Summer (7th solar term), Grain Full (8th solar term), Grain in Ear (9th solar term), Summer Solstice (10th solar term), Slight Heat (11th solar term), Great Heat (12th solar term), Beginning of Autumn (13th solar term), Limit of Heat (14th solar term), White Dew (15th solar term), Autumnal Equinox (16th solar term), Cold Dew (17th solar term), Frost's descent (18th solar term), Beginning of Winter (19th solar term), Slight Snow (20th solar term), Great Snow (21st solar term), Winter Solstice (22nd solar term), Slight Cold (23rd solar term), and Great Cold (24th solar term).
* writing brush: also called Chinese brush or brush for short, which is used for writing or painting, invented or renovated by Tien Meng (259 B.C.- 210 B.C.), a general in the Ch'in dynasty. It is one of the four treasures in a Chinese study, the other three stationeries being ink, paper and inkslab.

上清宝鼎诗二首
Celestial Tripod, Two Poems

其 一

人生烛上花，
光灭巧妍尽。
春风绕树头，
日与化工进。
只知雨露贪，
不闻零落近。
我昔飞骨时，
惨见当涂坟。
青松霭朝霞，
缥缈山下村。
既死明月魄，
无复玻璃魂。
念此一脱洒，
长啸祭昆仑。
醉著鸾皇衣，
星斗俯可扪。

No. 1

Life's like a snuff of candlelight;
Soon vanishes the glory bright.
A spring breeze blows around the tree;
All things change as Nature can be.
To dewy flowers don't cling so nigh;

Before long they'll wither and die.
In my dream I'm blown by an air
Into my Tangt'u Grave over there.
When pines out of hazy clouds show,
A mountain village looms below.
All will dim like the moon does wane;
None can with his glass soul remain.
One should be freed, at this I ween,
And with a howl I face Mt. Queen.
Drunk, I don phoenix plumage grand
And deign to stroke the stars by hand.

* Tangt'u Grave: Pai Li's tomb in present-day Tangt'u, Anhui Province. How Pai Li could foretell his grave would be in Tangt'u remains a mystery. According to one of Pai Li's granddaughters, Pai Li had expressed his desire of making the Green Hill at a short distance southeast of Great Peace (Taip'ing-fu) his last resting place, so his tomb was moved to the north side of the Green Hill in 818.
* glass soul: a transparent or crystal state of mind. Glass may have been introduced into China from Egypt in the T'ang dynasty.
* Mt. Queen: Mt. Kunlun if transliterated, is the one of the most sacred mountains in China. It starts from the eastern Pamir Plateau, stretches across New Land (Hsinchiang) and Tibet, and extends to Blue Sea (Ch'inghai), with an average altitude of 5,500 – 6,000 meters. In Chinese mythology, Mt. Queen is where Mother West dwells.

其 二

朝披梦泽云，
笠钓青茫茫。
寻丝得双鲤，
中有三元章。
篆字若丹蛇，
逸势如飞翔。
归来问天老，
奥义不可量。
金刀割青素，
灵文烂煌煌。
咽服十二镮，
想见仙人房。
暮跨紫鳞去，
海气侵肌凉。
龙子善变化，
化作梅花妆。
赠我累累珠，
靡靡明月光。
劝我穿绛缕，
系作裙间裆。
挹子以携去，
谈笑闻遗香。

No. 2

At dawn I don a Dream-Cloud hue,
And begin to fish by the blue.
I catch a pair of carps aligned;

A note in the stomach I find.
The scripts look like a red snake spry,
So vivid as if they would fly.
To inquire, to Sky Old I'd go;
The meaning's too profound to know.
With a knife I cut their skin fine;
The characters like spirits shine.
Behold, twelve rings swallowed inside,
Much like a bower for a fair bride.
Now scraping off the purple scales,
I feel, chill to my skin prevails.
They change, as they are dragons' sons,
Into plum blossoms that she dons.
And I have many pearls so bright,
Like smiling Luna shedding light.
I should bunch them with a red string;
So that on my belt they can swing.
Now I strut with a sway of arm;
My laugh stirs up a draught of balm.

* Dream-Bog hue: sunlit mist arising from Dream and Cloud, which were two swamps, the former being north of the Long River and the latter south of it, that is, near Lake Cavehall.
* a pair of carps: a symbol of a letter wherein to express one's love or missing, also the alias of a letter, because in ancient China a letter was usually written on silk and the silk was then bound in two slabs of bamboo, which were carved like a pair of fish.
* snake: an ophidian reptile, having a greatly elongated, smooth and cold scaly body, no limbs, and a specialized swallowing apparatus, a symbol of indifference, malevolence, cattiness, and craftiness in Chinese culture.
* Sky Old: Lord Yellow's advisor as is recorded in *Bamboo Book Annals* and *Lord Yellow Cartshaft*.
* carp: fresh water food fish (*Ciprinus carpiao*) of China, now widely distributed in Europe and America, a mascot in Chinese culture, symbolizing great success and

harmony. An idiom "a carp jumping over the Dragon Gate" means climbing up the social ladder or succeeding in the imperial civil service examination.
* dragon: Though variously understood as a large reptile, a marine monster, a jackal and so on in Western culture, it has been esteemed as a fabulous serpent-like giant winged animal that can change its girth and length, a totem of the Chinese nation and a symbol of benevolence and sovereignty in Chinese culture.
* pearl: a lustrous, calcareous concretion deposited in layers around a central nucleus in the shells of various mollusks, and largely used as a gem, regarded as a treasure or given as a gift to represent love and friendship.
* Luna: the moon, the goddess of the moon and of months in Roman mythology, and in Chinese culture the imperial concubine of Lord Alarm (2,480 B.C.- 2,345 B.C.), one of five mythical emperors in prehistorical China. Luna or the moon is an important image in Chinese literature as it can give rise to many associations such as solitude, purity, brightness and happy reunions.

白　微　时

白微时，募县小吏，入令卧内，尝驱牛经堂下，令妻怒，将加诘责，白亟以诗谢云

素面倚栏钩，
娇声出外头。
若非是织女，
何得问牵牛。

When I Was Low

When I was low, I was employed as a county clerk. I once drove an ox outside the bedroom of the magistrate. His wife got angry and would blame me. So I tried to beg her pardon with this poem.

By the net hook shows your fair face;
Your voice comes out, seemingly coy.
If you are not the weaving maid,
Why should you ask the herding boy?

* the weaving maid: Weaver Maid, Vega, in Chinese mythology, a fairy who stole out of the sky and fell in love with Cowherd, an orphan, and was married to him. When discovered, Weaver Maid was relentlessly taken away and kept away from Cowherd by Queen Mother, who made the Silver River (the Milky Way) with her hair pin. They could only meet once a year at Magpie Bridge magpies made for them on the seventh day of the seventh moon.
* the herding boy: Cowherd, Weaver's husband in the mythology. Pai Li was playfully referring to himself playing the part of the herding boy and taking the magistrate's wife as Weaver, his lover.

夜 宿 山 寺

危楼高百尺，
手可摘星辰。
不敢高声语，
恐惊天上人。

Putting Up for the Night in a Mountain Temple

The tower is like a towering peak,
One may pick up a star on high.
In a loud voice I dare not speak,
Lest I frighten those in the sky.

* a mountain temple: a temple in a district in today's Hupei Province. It was so isolated from the outside world that this poem of Pai Li's, written on a painted board which was left on a beam of the ceiling, remained unmolested for centuries until it was discovered by a local magistrate.

题戴老酒店

戴老黄泉下，
还应酿大春。
夜台无李白，
沽酒与何人？

An Inscription for Mr. Tai's Wineshop

In Hades now you fare;
As e'er Big Spring you brew.
Without Pai Li down there,
Whom do you sell wine to?

* Hades: the abode of the dead, and a euphemism for the netherworld or hell. It is called Yellow Spring in Chinese culture, because water deep down earth is yellow, and Yellow Spring belongs in the Nine Hells and Nine Springs in Wordist terms.
* Big Spring: the name of a kind of wine, famous for its good quality.
* Pai Li: our author, the author being translated. He is as much legend as history, whom we seem to know a lot but actually know little. He was born in A.D. 701, as many historians agree and died in A.D. 762, as was recorded. Saliently, he was a poet, then a drunkard, then a swordsman, a traveler, a recluse, and so on. God of Wine he called himself, Fallen Immortal his friend called him, and Fairy of Poetry we all call him. He is a miracle and mystery, as his poems may reveal.

折 荷 有 赠

涉江玩秋水，
爱此红蕖鲜。
攀荷弄其珠，
荡漾不成圆。
佳人彩云里，
欲赠隔远天。
相思无因见，
惆怅凉风前。

Plucking a Lotus Bloom as a Gift

I row, the chill water I play,
And I love red lotus blooms gay.
I pluck a leaf and touch a bead;
To be a disc a splash can't lead.
A beauty in the clouds looms shy;
Give her one? I'm barred by the sky!
This belle I miss but cannot hold;
I sigh long before the wind cold.

* lotus: one of the various plants of the waterlily family, characterized by their large floating round leaves and showy flowers, especially the white or pink Asian lotus, used as a religious symbol in Hinduism and Buddhism. In Chinese culture, it is a symbol of purity and elegance, unsoiled though out of soil, so clean with all leaves green, is is a common image in Chinese literature, as two lines of a lyric by Hsiu Ouyang (A.D. 1007 - A.D. 1072) read:"A thunder brings rain to the wood and pool, / The rain hushes the lotus, drips cool."

别 匡 山

晓峰如画碧参差，
藤影风摇拂槛垂。
野径来多将犬伴，
人间归晚带樵随。
看云客倚啼猿树，
洗钵僧临失鹤池。
莫怪无心恋清境，
已将书剑许明时。

Good-bye to Mt. Square

The scenic peaks at dawn roll high and low;
The rattan shade on the rails wind does blow.
Many walk with their dogs on the trail wild;
Farmers return at dusk with firewood piled.
Monkeys whine on the tree whereby I stand;
Monks wash their bowl at Pool of CraneStrand.
Do not blame me forleaving this quiet clime;
I'll give my books and sword to the good time.

* rattan: the long, tough, flexible stem of a palm (genera Calamus and Daemonorops) growing in Asia, Africa and Australia, which can be used as material for the making of chairs and a variety of other furniture.
* the rails: referring to the rails of Grand Brightness Temple on Mt. Square.
* Mt. Square: about 25 kilometers from Green Lotus, Pai Li's hometown, and Pai Li studied and practiced swordplay for ten years in the Mt. Square Academy here.
* Pool of Crane Strand: the pool where cranes were raised according to the *Annals of Bright County*.

译 者 简 介

赵彦春教授致力于中华经典典籍的翻译和传播。他持表征之神杖,舞锐利之弧矢,启翻译范式之革命,将诗歌之"不可译"变为"可译";将"译之所失"变为"译之所得";将中华五千年的语言、哲学、诗学和美学的智慧融为一体,进行大胆尝试而细腻创新;他坚持译诗如诗,译经如经,从音韵形式、思想内容和文化意蕴上完美诠释了音美、形美和意美的统一;他相信语言与宇宙同构,将翻译的"诗学空间"不断延伸和拓展。

为了讲好"中国故事",引领中国文化"走出去",他带领一批志同道合的专业人士兢兢业业,孜孜不倦,锐意进取。从编辑、出版经典译著到举办国学外译研修班,从召开经典外译与国际传播学术研讨会、举办中华文化国际翻译大赛到创办 Translating China(《翻译中国》)国际期刊,他和同仁将忙碌的身影融入到了中华文化复兴的背景之中。

他带着"赵彦春国学经典英译系列"等一大批优秀的翻译成果走向世界,向世界展示中华文明的无尽魅力。

他无愧为中华典籍传统文化的传承者和传播者。

About the Translator

Professor Yanchun Chao devotes himself to the translation and transmission of Chinese classics. To inherit the traditional Chinese culture, he holds the divine scepter of Representation and sways the sharpness of bow and arrow to initiate a paradigm revolution out of fallacies, turning "untranslatability" of poetry into "translatability", "losses of translation" into "gains of translation", integrating the wisdom of five thousand years of Chinese language, philosophy, poetics and aesthetics to make bold attempts and exquisite innovations; he insists on translating Poesie into Poesie and Classic into Classic, perfectly interpreting the beauty of sound, form and sense from prosodic features, ideological contents and cultural implications; he also believes that language is isomorphic to the universe and constantly expands the "Poetic Space" of translation.

To tell good "Chinese stories" and lead them to "go global", he guides a group of like-minded specialists to work with diligence and fortitude, editing and publishing classic translations, convening seminars on English translation of Chinese culture, holding conferences on Classic Translation and International Communication, organizing "CC CUP" International Chinese Culture Translation Contest and editing an international journal *Translating China*, their busy figures silhouetted against the background of the revival of traditional Chinese culture.

With "Yanchun Chao's English Translation Series of Chinese Classics" going global, he shows to the world the endless appeal of the Chinese civilization.

He is a true inheritor and promoter of Chinese classics and traditional Chinese culture.